The Queen's Spy

Ruth S. Daigneault

Also by Ruth S. Daigneault

Novels

The 13th Guest

Nonfiction

The Last Journey - Going Home

(with L. Paul Daigneault)

Writing as Ruth S. Rogers

Fifteen Dinner Theatre Comedy Plays including

The Grand Reopening of Cin's Saloon

The Wedding

S. S. Gigantic

Whispering Pines

The Pink Flamingo

The Queen's Spy by Ruth S. Daigneault

ISBN: 978-0-9918053-5-8

For my wonderful husband, Paul, who shows me every day what love is. and my three wonderful children, Debbie, Heather and Tony, my shining stars through all the years.

Contents

Chapter 1

Boar's Head Alehouse, Littleton, England 1584

The men in the Boar's Head cheered and raised their earthenware pots to the young man as he put his fiddle down on the table. The barmaid, her pretty face glowing from hurrying between tables, placed a mug of ale in front of him.

"There you are, luv," Annie said, giving him a wink.

Jeremy Hawkins thanked her and held his pot aloft, returning the salute of the other patrons. The locals resumed their two main interests - talking and drinking. Noisy conversation and laughter filled the dimly lit, smoky room. For the benefit of any who might be watching, Jeremy gazed fixedly at the liquid in front of him as if he found something singularly fascinating in the dark depths.

As the heavy wooden door swung open, a gust of cold night air heralded the arrival of David Lancaster, his slim frame well muffled up against the chill of February in England. He stamped his feet, threw back his cloak and called a greeting to several friends. Alfie Fitzhugh, owner of the establishment, looked up from behind the bar and gave David the extra warm smile he reserved for special friends.

Ducking under a couple of lanterns, David crossed the room to the blazing fire beside Jeremy's table. To everyone else, Lancaster was a jovial young man given to wenching and drinking, with nary a serious thought in his head, but Jeremy knew him better than most. Never would anyone suspect he was a loyal and faithful subject of Queen Elizabeth, spying for her that she might be kept safe in the troubled days of 1584.

David rubbed his hands together as he held them out to the warmth. He turned to Jeremy and spoke heartily while rumpling the young man's carefully brushed brown hair. "How is old addle-headed raglegs tonight?"

"Fine, David, just fine." Jeremy grinned at him, taking no offence at the reference to his crippled legs. For the last seven years of the scant nineteen years he had been on earth, Jeremy had been the brunt of many jeers and jibes. In this case, however, David's name-calling was just part of the act to reinforce the illusion of his stupidity.

"One over here, Annie," David called, as he sat down beside Jeremy and stretched his legs out to the fire. Conversation in the room returned to normal pitch.

When Annie brought his ale, David took a big swallow. "Aaaaah, that warms a man's insides." Holding the pot in front of his mouth, David quietly addressed Jeremy by the name used to hide his real identity. "What have you got for me, Michael?"

"This is a well-organized one, David. In six days, they will attempt to free Mary Stuart and set her on the throne. The bastards discussed their scheme here this afternoon, as usual not worrying at all about the stupid cripple. Queen Bess's two chamber guards, the ones who come on at midnight, are in on the plot. They will pass the assassin into the room to kill the Queen. In the meantime, four others will overpower the sentries guarding Mary Stuart at Sheffield and bring her to Windsor Castle."

David drew in a breath. "That's major news, Michael," he said quietly before downing his drink. He turned to look at the bar called loudly, "Let's have another one, Annie, and one for pudding legs too." He leaned his head toward Jeremy.

"Spencer and Cartwright, the plotters today, will be waiting at Windsor as well, acting as lookouts. I tell you, David, they're really well set up this time. They mean to succeed in establishing Mary on the throne."

"We'll get them, don't worry." David looked over his left shoulder. "Who's that scoundrel over there? The one near the door with his cap pulled down? I'm sure he's watching you."

"Here you are, Michael." Annie placed their mugs on the table.

"Thank you, Annie." He waited until Annie walked away before answering David. "Name's Forsythe. Unsavoury sort. Hangs about the docks."

David leaned across the table and shielded his mouth with his hand. "I don't like the looks of him or the way he's watching you. Jemmy, be careful. You can't fight or run away like the rest of us."

"I'll be all right. Just get the message through to the Queen so she can protect herself. Remember, six days from now."

"I understand." David took a long pull of his drink. "Meanwhile, it's time you got out of here. Your brother, John, left orders before he set sail that you were to leave upon discovery of any major information, and the good God above knows this is major indeed. When this latest plot is foiled, people might become suspicious and John would have my head if anything happened to you." In his booming voice, David continued, "How's about a tune, pudding-legs? Play something jolly before I go."

Others joined in. "Play us a tune. Come on there, Mikey."

Jeremy picked up his fiddle and began playing a lively sailor's ditty. The men stamped their feet and clapped their hands in time to the music. When he finished, Jeremy slipped the fiddle under the table, the signal he used to let David know he had no more information to pass along.

David leaned his face close to Jeremy's. "Right then. Remember what I said. Get away as soon as you can - tonight if possible. I hope to see you again in this lifetime and not wait till the next."

"You're a good friend, David. Come for a visit some time."

David grinned. "I will. But I must leave now. Godspeed on your journey home." Tossing down his ale, David stood and made his way to the door.

Jeremy decided to wait until closing time before asking Alfie to help him get ready for departure. He thought about how wonderful it would be to return to the family home in Nottinghamshire after an absence of six months, although his sister, Cathy, would not yet have returned from her etiquette schooling in France and Italy. Jeremy smiled to himself as he wondered if the tutors were having any luck turning the fourteen year-old tomboy into a dignified young lady. He decided that would be highly unlikely this soon, and would no doubt take the entire three years she was scheduled to remain there to render any change in the strong-willed young girl.

Alfie made the call to drink up, and the patrons obliged before taking their leave of the Boar's Head. Amidst all the jovial farewells and general confusion, no one noticed the man who slipped into the room at the back of the alehouse.

Jeremy waited until the pots were gathered up, tables wiped and floor swept before telling Alfie that he had to get ready for departure and requesting the use of a cart.

"Sorry we are to be losing you, Mikey. I suppose I couldn't convince you to stay a little longer?"

"Your hospitality has been wonderful, Alfie, but I must be off."

"Right-o. You'll be wantin' to get to yer room now."

"Yes, please."

Alfie easily lifted up the young man with his powerful arms, developed in years past by local fight matches. He took Jeremy to his room and settled him in a chair.

"I'll just be off to ready the cart," Alfie said.

Jeremy nodded and began removing his belongings from the dresser. At a sudden rustling noise from behind him, Jeremy turned his head in time to see a figure emerge from behind the armoire. A strong arm locked itself under his chin almost totally blocking off his airway. Jeremy struggled to pull the arm away, but his head was forced back and he found himself looking into the surly face of Fred Forsythe.

"You miserable slimy sea serpent. I know what you're up to - you and your simpleton act." With that, he punched Jeremy in the side of the head with his right fist, knocking the young man to the floor. Free from the assailant's grip, Jeremy gulped in some air. "I been watching you. I seen you listening to me and my mateys talking tonight. Thought you could get away with it, didn't you?" the coarse voice continued.

"What?"

Forsythe stood over Jeremy legs apart and hands on his hips. "Did the captain offer you a reward for turning us in?"

"What captain? I don't know what you're talking about."

"Stop pretending you don't know about our plans!" Forsythe kicked him in the ribs. "Maybe that'll help your memory, you no-good spying son of a she-devil."

Jeremy groaned.

The door swung open. The smile on Alfie's face changed to anger as he took in the scene. Without hesitation, he stepped forward and landed a heavy blow to Forsythe's chin, which sent him falling backwards into the armoire. The crack of his head was loud and Forsythe's body crumpled to the floor where Death claimed him instantly.

"Good riddance to bad rubbish," Alfie said. He turned to Jeremy. "How are ye, lad? Anything broken?"

"I don't think so," Jeremy said, "thanks to your opportune arrival. How did you come to be back so swiftly?"

Alfie lifted Jeremy onto the chair before answering. "I forgot to ask if you wanted someone to go with you right to your home - wherever that is. First time I've ever been glad of my forgetfulness."

"Well, I'm certainly glad of it, Alfie, else I might not be sitting here talking to you. I don't know what got into him."

"What did he want?"

"I really don't know. He was raving on about a reward from some captain for turning him in." Jeremy rubbed the side of his head.

"Likely some mutiny or other. Those blokes are always complaining. Doesn't matter none. He was a disgrace to humanity. Tried to assault our Annie a while back. I should've killed him then." Alfie kicked the inert Forsythe for good measure.

"What are you going to do with the body?"

"You don't need to concern yourself none with that. Ain't nobody around here going to miss that rat. You finish packing while

I get him out of the room before he starts stinking up the place." Alfie hoisted Forsythe's body over his shoulder and started to the door.

"Wait! I never answered your question."

"Oh, right. Damn memory!" Alfie chuckled. "And your wish?"

"Someone to accompany to the coach stop would be fine so he can return your cart. I prefer to travel the rest of the way on my own, but thank you for your offer."

"You're welcome, lad."

As Jeremy finished his packing, he thought how right David had been to warn him to get out of here. Frown lines appeared on his forehead as he wondered about his friend's safety. It was impossible to know if Forsythe had suspected David as well.

By the time Alfie returned, Jeremy was packed and ready to go.

"Alfie, you've been a wonderful friend to me and I can't imagine how I would have managed without your help."

"Twas my pleasure, lad. Ye are a fine young man, and I'm sure there are good things in store for your future - something fancier than the Boar's Head. Let's away."

With ease, Alfie carried Jeremy out to the cart, settled him comfortably with a rug on his knees, and offered his hand in final farewell. "God keep ye safe, lad. I hope we see you again some time."

"I would like that, Alfie. You are a great friend. Farewell."

"You, Dickie, see the horse gets brushed down when you get back, and settle her down for the night."

"Yes sir. You can count on me, sir."

As the cart rumbled away, Jeremy turned back once to wave a final farewell to Alfie Fitzhugh, barely visible in the darkness of the night. He knew he could never come this way again. The thought made him a little sad, for Alfie and Annie had become good friends, a commodity hard to find in any lifetime.

Chapter 2

Windsor Castle, Six Days Later

"Damn bloody cold night, and crawling through that wet grass didn't help," Spencer said.

"Aye, but nice and dark. A good night for a murder," Cartwright chuckled under his breath. Two other men nodded agreement.

"Best not be talking anymore. The guards'll be lettin' us in any minute."

The men huddled together near a side door.

"What's taking them so long?" Spencer said. "They should have been down by now."

"Listen," Cartwright hissed.

A slight noise came from inside the door. It slowly opened.

"About time you let us in," Spencer said. He stepped through, quickly followed by the other three. A light shone dimly from around a corner a few feet ahead.

"Move forward," ordered the person holding the door.

"Right. Come on, boys," Cartwright said, heading toward the light.

As they rounded the corner, Cartwright stopped suddenly. Directly ahead, a dozen armed guards blocked the passage, swords appearing to be on fire as they reflected the flames of the wall torches.

"What ..."

Confused, the men looked at each other, turned quickly, only to discover their way was blocked by more guards. They had barely time to register what was happening, before their bodies crumpled to the floor, run through with several sword blades.

"Get them out of here and see the blood is cleaned up off the floor," said Blanche Parry, the woman who had opened the door. She did not wait for her order to be carried out but hurried away upstairs to the Queen's chambers. The Queen's new personal chamber guards let her in. She rushed to Elizabeth's side.

"Your Majesty," she said, trying to catch her breath.

"Speak, Blanche. Tell me what has happened."

"All has been taken care of, Your Majesty. The would-be assassins have met their just reward. You may rest easy this night."

Elizabeth's eyes sparkled. "How many were there?"

"Four, not counting your two chamber guards who were dispatched earlier."

Elizabeth hugged her friend. "They have done well, but we must always be on our guard. Thank you for being there and bringing me such speedy word."

"I'm sure we shall all rest easier in our beds tonight, knowing those blackguards have been disposed of."

Elizabeth began to pace. "These Papists and their never-ending plots are becoming much too bold. I think I will soon have to make some other plans." Queen Elizabeth turned to her friend and lady-in-waiting. "Not tonight, though. I am very tired and have had quite enough excitement. Let us retire to my bedchamber. This has been a long day."

Chapter 3

Windsor Castle, February 1587

Not for the first time Francis Drake looked at the 53 year-old monarch and wondered at the way she seemed like two different people: the one delighted in his recounts of pillage and slaughter and had her cousin Mary imprisoned for twenty years and ultimately murdered a mere two weeks ago; the other a gracious lady who gently played her music, listened to the concerns of her people and extensively helped to develop the arts, even going so far as to lend her presence to a recent play produced by The Lord Chamberlain's Men, starring an up and coming young actor, Will Shakespeare.

At the moment, she was pacing up and down, her elegant, gold-threaded gown swishing against the floor, a frown creasing the white paint on her face. No doubt Elizabeth was worried about the Spanish and the possibility of another assassination plot, despite Francis' assurance that steps had been taken to ensure her safety and that of England. Not for a moment did Francis think she was regretting refusing Philip's many offers of marriage.

"Your Majesty, you must trust me again as you have done in the past. John Hawkins and I are working out a plan to put someone in place as a spy in the most appropriate location, as we did three years ago. We are quite certain the plan will work and that the young man whose services we intend to secure will accept. As the locale is frequented by those rebels who would seek to plot against your Majesty, he will be able to provide us quickly with valuable information regarding Philip's actions."

"Francis, we cannot quarrel with your judgment. You have swelled the English coffers beyond anything we expected and we have always relied on you, so we must now trust what you are saying. You believe this person to be totally trustworthy and reliable?"

"Indeed he is, Your Majesty. He has served Your Majesty well previously, for he it was who uncovered the plot to free Mary four years ago, as I mentioned. "

"Will he not be recognized if he returns to the same place?"

"Quite possibly, Your Majesty, as he was attacked previously. That is why we will send him elsewhere."

"A reasonable plan. And what is the name of this individual whom you expect to offer his services yet again?"

"Begging Your Majesty's pardon, for your own safety it is better you do not know this, but I can most assuredly guarantee he is a loyal subject and will have to give up much of his personal life to devote to our needs."

"Ah. We see. And is he in place now?"

"No. We must first make sure all possible contingencies are covered, and when all is set on our end, John Hawkins will contact the man to request his assistance. We anticipate he will be in place before the summer."

"Can we do anything to assist this young man?"

"That is most kind of you, Your Majesty, but all arrangements are being taken care of by John."

"But we wish to do something." Elizabeth opened the lid of a small jar. "Give him this to keep as a thank you and tell him should he ever have need of assistance from us, he should send this by messenger." She handed Drake a huge ruby ring surrounded by emeralds.

"Your Majesty! I don't think ..." He stopped at the imperious look coming from under raised eyebrows. "I am sure he will be very honoured to receive your gracious gift and offer of help."

"Good. And perhaps an additional reward after he completes his mission?"

"A most kind and generous offer, Your Majesty, although I'm sure he will expect no reward."

"We shall discuss that in the future,"

"As you wish, Your Majesty."

"Thank you, Francis, for making the arrangements. We do trust you implicitly."

"Thank you, Your Majesty."

"We want Phillip squashed once and for all, you understand."

"I understand your wishes perfectly. It shall be as you desire. You have my word. In a few days I will set sail for Cadiz and deal a mighty blow to Philip's fleet."

"Thank you, Francis. What I would give to see the look on Philip's face when he gets word of your attack." Elizabeth chuckled. "Godspeed on your voyage, Francis. We look forward to receiving a full and detailed account of your victorious trip."

"It will be my pleasure to deliver the tale, Your Majesty."

"Oh, before you leave, you might like to take in a viewing of the play of that strange young man, Will Shakespeare. His behaviour in public, we understand is somewhat bizarre, however his talent as an actor cannot be denied."

"I shall see if that is possible. Thank you for thinking of me."

"One must encourage the arts in young people, Francis. We are a civilized country, after all. And now, we wish to be alone. You may go. God be with you."

"Your Majesty." Francis rose and backed out of the room.

Chapter 4

Hawkesbury Manor, February 1587

Several days after Francis Drake had his conversation with Queen Elizabeth, David Lancaster rode up the long drive to Hawkins Manor.

He was greeted by a young boy who had run up from the stables. Jumping down, Lancaster tossed him a coin and the reins and dusted off his clothes before heading the stairs to the front door. His knock was answered by a middle-aged woman whose solemn countenance did not register any delight in this intrusion.

"Good afternoon, my dear Mrs. Pedley," David said, with a slight bow. "Would Jeremy be at home today?"

"Yes." She glanced to a door on her left. "I'll see if ..."

"Please do not trouble yourself, most gracious lady. I'm sure you have vastly more important things to do than trouble yourself to announce your humble servant. Besides, I wish to surprise Jeremy." Without waiting for a reply, David moved past the astonished woman and opened the door at which she had looked.

"Jeremy, you old stick! How are you?" David said, extending his hand.

"David!" Jeremy quickly laid aside the book he had been reading.

"He pushed right past me, Master Jeremy."

"Quite all right, Mrs. Pedley. David is an old friend."

She sniffed audibly. "Doesn't give a person a right to push his way in."

"Come, come, Mrs. Pedley. You see? I told you it would be all right. And if not, you and I would have run away together," David said, bowing low.

Jeremy thought he noticed a slight smile on Mrs. Pedley's face before she exited. It was hard for anyone to resist David's charm.

"Still the ladies' man, David. It's wonderful to see you. And I'm fine. Sit, sit, sit. What brings you all the way to Nottinghamshire?"

"What? You don't believe I came just to visit an old friend?"

"Well, it has been three years, and here you are out of the blue. It does make one curious. But I'm pleased as punch to see you. Will you have a drink? Something to eat?"

"Perhaps a drink."

"If you don't mind helping yourself. Everything is over on the sideboard."

"Of course. Thank you." As he poured, David continued, "So how have you been since the days of the Boar's Head? I understand there was a bit of a set-to before you got away."

"Yes. A bloke was on to me - in fact, I think you mentioned him the night you came. Forsythe? Seedy-looking sort. I think he suspected something because he said he knew I was going to report his plans to a captain, which made me think immediately of John. Fortunately, Alfie came to my rescue, or I might not be sitting here today."

David pulled up a chair close to Jeremy. "That's pretty much what Alfie said."

"How is he?"

"I don't go often, but he was quite well on my last visit about six months ago."

"He's a good man. I miss those folks." David looked like he was going to interrupt. "Yes, yes, I know. Can't go back, and, of course, I haven't. And what about you? What have you been up to - if you can tell me, that is."

"That's actually what I've come to talk to you about." David hesitated. "Jeremy, have you heard about Queen Mary's execution?"

"Execution?! No. When did that happen?"

"A couple of weeks ago. After all these years, Her Majesty decided to have her beheaded."

"I never thought she'd do such a thing." A frown creased his forehead. "I daresay that has caused quite a stir among the Papists."

"Absolutely. Scuffles have popped up here and there."

Jeremy looked at his friend. "Not surprising. But I sense this has caused you some distress, although I'm not sure why. Were some of your friends killed?"

"No, nothing like that." David took in a deep breath. "Jeremy, early last year, I was sent to Spain to do a little, um, investigative work, so to speak. While in Spain, I met a very beautiful young woman and ... well, the long and short of it is, we fell in love. In fact, we are betrothed."

"Congratulations! That's wonderful news. So who is the lucky lady who has won your heart?"

"Her name is Isabella Perez. She is a dazzling beauty, full of wit and charm, intelligent in many ways, and of good family."

"Your Isabella sounds like a real treasure." Jeremy looked closely at David. "So ... why does something seem to be troubling you?"

David sighed. "Isabella is a Catholic."

"Oh."

"Exactly. To become engaged, I had to join her church - not that I had any real objection. There is so little difference between the two religions. We are to be married soon, but with the death of Mary, the animosity between our countries has intensified to a point which makes it nearly impossible for me to get back to Spain, and, understandably, Isabella has no desire to come here."

"Quite so. Is there something I can do for you?"

"Not really, although I do have a request, which I feel I must make, seeing as we are on opposing sides in a way ..."

"David, your choice of religion doesn't matter to me. You are my friend. I am sure you are still loyal to Queen Elizabeth, no matter what church you attend." He gazed searchingly at his friend. "You are, aren't you?"

"As much as I can be, Jeremy."

"I realize spying for Elizabeth will be out of the question, but ..."

"Indeed. And recently I've heard your brother John and Francis Drake are working hard on some new scheme to take down Philip and his empire. I'm afraid they may ask me to help, which I cannot do any more, especially in light of my marriage into the Perez family. On top of that, Isabella's father is a General in the Spanish Army, and isn't exactly happy at her choice of husband. He watches my activities pretty closely. If I must go to live in Spain, and I must, I fail to see how I can still be loyal to England's monarch, and most certainly cannot continue spying on her behalf."

"Have you told this to John?"

"Not in person. He's been away with Drake at the times when I was in London, but I did leave a message at his house."

"I understand. Laying the spying aside as it is obviously impossible, do you not think an Englishman's an Englishman, no matter where he resides?"

"Quite possibly, but during a discussion on loyalties with Isabella, she quoted what Jesus said in the Bible, 'render unto Caesar that which is Caesar's', and I will be living in Spain ..." David let his sentence hang.

"But deep in your heart, you are still an Englishman, right?"

"Yes, of course." He tried to keep the lack of confidence out of his voice.

"It's doubtful I will be seeing John either. So what I can do for you?"

"It's just that ... if John, or someone, comes to ask you to, um ... get involved in whatever plan they are proposing ... I'm asking that you refuse. As your friend."

"Ask ME??!! What makes you think they will come back to me again? The last time ended in a bit of a shambles."

"Even so, as a friend, I'm just requesting if they ask, you refuse."

Jeremy chuckled. "David, I'm puzzled why you are worried, but I think you are fretting for nothing. I haven't seen John in months, and I sincerely doubt he, or anyone else, has any intention of trying to involve me in some kind of scheme ... which, incidentally, you are not even sure exists. I certainly haven't heard anything, and very much doubt I will."

"Just the same, I would be happier knowing you are safe here at Hawkins Manor."

"You seem truly worried. Is there something more you're not telling me?"

David hesitated. "No, no. We're friends, that's all, and I'd like to have you meet Isabella once all this hostility is settled.

"Come now. Don't look so serious." Jeremy smiled. "I will look forward to meeting the delightful Isabella, and quite likely, a large brood of little Lancasters."

"Not too many, I hope, especially if they are as bad as we were as youngsters."

"Will you stay on a few days?"

"Thank you, Jeremy, for your gracious offer, but I must refuse."

"Ah ... the siren's call is echoing in your head."

"More like a ship's whistle. I am leaving for Spain in a few days, so must decline your invitation and be on my way."

"You're leaving already? Cathy will be sorry to have missed you. She is off visiting some friends."

David stood. "Please give that irrepressible young lady a hug for me."

"I will do so."

"Jeremy," David frowned, "I love you like a brother. Please remember what I've said and stay safe."

"You have turned into an old worry-wart, David. If that's what love and marriage do to you, I think I'll bypass both." Jeremy laughed.

David clapped Jeremy's shoulder. "Take care, my friend."

"And you. Safe travels and all my best wishes for a very happy marriage."

"Thanks, Jeremy." David turned back at the door. "Farewell."

Jeremy raised his arm. "Till we meet again."

Through the front window, he watched David ride away and smiled as he thought of David's upcoming marriage. He wondered if David really could stop his flirting ways and assume the role of faithful husband.

Jeremy picked up the book he had put aside when David arrived, but found thoughts of what David had said about the increasing tension between England and Spain kept intruding themselves into the midst of a paper entitled 'Proofs of Reincarnation'. Once more, he laid the book down and gazed thoughtfully into space.

Chapter 5

Hawkesbury Manor, May 1587

Has there ever been a time when the world was truly at peace? It would seem not. But no matter the battles that rage for possessions or territories, the rich who wish to acquire more power, or individuals who seek political gain, for those not directly involved in the conflict, ordinary life goes on undisturbed. The death of Mary, Queen of Scots, and the escalating animosity of England and Spain, while discussed quietly in the pubs of London, had little impact on the rural inhabitants of the seafaring nation of England. People ate, slept, laughed and loved and continued living a normal life. Such is the way it was in May of the year of our Lord 1587, at the Hawkins Manor House situated in the beautiful green countryside of Nottinghamshire.

The land on which the house stood had been deeded to an ancestral Hawkins by Henry VII for his valour during the Battle of Bosworth in saving Henry's life from the attacking army of Richard III. The manor itself had been built with monies provided by Henry from the English coffers.

Through astute money handling, the family's wealth had increased over the years, allowing the members to maintain a lifestyle befitting the stately home in which they lived.

In a large apartment off the great hall, Jeremy Hawkins read the cryptic letter for the third time with a puzzled look on his face, and pondered what his brother John had in mind. Why was he arriving in the middle of the night and why must no one be told?

"There you sit with your head in those stuffy old books!" This admonition was followed by a rush of swirling skirts and two slim arms thrown around Jeremy's neck. "Ever since Father died, you've been a real stick-in-the-mud!"

"Faith! You are enough to scare me half to death my dear sister," Jeremy said, quickly shoving the letter under a book. "I wonder if you will ever be able to enter the room like a lady rather than a full-fledged storm," he said good-naturedly. "Apparently, more than three years in France and Italy had little effect on you. You were supposed to come back a proper lady."

"Piffle! I don't see why ladies can't run, whistle or do anything else they please, Jeremy. Just because I can ride a horse better than most men, doesn't mean I'm not a lady. I'm quite grown up, and I will be positively ancient on my birthday next year. How am I ever going to be able to survive being that old?"

Jeremy Hawkins laughed. "I hardly think being 18 makes you an old woman, Catherine."

Catherine sighed. "Oh, but it does. I have friends who were married at 16, and one even has a child. Not that I want to have children, mind. At least not right away. I want to have some adventures first. Don't you think it would be wonderful to have adventures, Jemmy?" Catherine stopped short. "Oh, I'm sorry, love. I know you can't have any real adventures," she said sadly, looking at his legs.

Jeremy smiled inwardly as he wondered what Catherine would think of his 'adventure' at The Boar's Head. "Being around you is adventure enough for me, Cathy. Just because I can't walk anywhere, doesn't mean I don't enjoy life. And my books give my mind plenty of 'adventures' as you call them."

"Piffle! Look at these!" she said, picking up a book. "'Living Forever' , 'Reincarnation', 'Manuscripts of the Ancients'. How can a book about old people give you a thrill?"

Jeremy laughed heartily. "Catherine, you will be the death of me! These books have nothing to do with old people."

"Then they shouldn't give them silly titles like that. Anyway, I'm going for a ride. Look," she said, turning his head to the left so he faced the open French doors. Daffodils, their brilliant yellow blooms dazzling in the bright April sun, nodded to a wayward breeze passing by.

"It's a beautiful day. You should be outside too. Would you like Richard to come and help you? He's probably in his workshop. I'll tell him to come get you. You can sit in the summerhouse and even take one of your dusty old books with you, although why you would want to is beyond me. Or maybe you could try to catch Mr. Getaway. Do you think any of us really want to catch him? I think we would miss him dreadfully. But I think he might be hungry, don't you? After all, he's been asleep all winter in the bottom of the pond. I'll send Richard in." Without waiting for a response, she raced out the door.

Jeremy sighed and shook his head. Trying to keep up with Catherine's conversation was like trying to catch the very elusive Mr. Getaway, the senior resident trout in the Hawkins Manor pond. But she was right. The day was lovely and it wouldn't hurt him to get outside for a bit. He rang the little bell on his desk, just as Richard Pedley came hurrying in from the outside doors.

"You rang?"

"Good lord, Richard, were you waiting about at the door?"

"No, but I came lickety-split from my workshop as ordered emphatically by your sister, who said, and I quote: "Jeremy needs to be got away from those stuffy old books he's reading. Take him out to the summerhouse." Now, you know as well as I do, Miss Catherine wants immediate action when she speaks."

Both young men laughed.

"Let me get you into this contraption." Richard lifted Jeremy easily and placed him on the small bench with wheels he had built a few years ago to give his friend some mobility.

"I pity the man who becomes her husband," Jeremy said. "She'll lead him a merry chase."

Richard smiled thoughtfully. "But, oh, what a pleasurable chase."

Jeremy eyed his friend and was about to speak, when a cough interrupted him.

"You wished to see me, Master Jeremy?

Jeremy glanced up at Evelyn Pedley standing in the hall doorway. Her dark brown hair was drawn back tightly from her face, revealing the close-set dark eyes, down-turned mouth and sharp, beaked nose which always reminded Jeremy of an owl. He raised his eyebrows and glanced sympathetically at Richard.

Mrs. Pedley gazed with little pleasure at the scene before her. It irked her that her son, vigorous and strong, would forever be a lackey to someone she considered a miserable excuse for a man. Not wishing to place her position in jeopardy, Evelyn Pedley concealed her true feelings most of the time, but, when unobserved, looked at Jeremy with scorn, bordering on antipathy.

"Ah yes. Please tell Mrs. Stewart we will be having our lunch in the summerhouse. I rather fancy a quail dish if she has any on hand. Richard, you will join Cathy and me, yes?"

After a quick glance at his mother, Richard nodded. Despite Jeremy's many assurances that, after growing up together, they were more friends than anything else, Richard always felt uncomfortable accepting such gestures in the presence of his mother.

"Good. For three then, Mrs. Pedley."

"Certainly." She left to give his instructions to the cook.

"Come now, Richard. Let us get to the summerhouse before Cathy comes back and gives us a tongue-lashing."

"Off we go," Richard said, pushing the wheeled bench to the doors.

Moving along the path toward the back of the estate, Jeremy drew in a deep breath. "Much as I hate to admit it, I think Catherine was right. I do need to get outside more often, and I suppose reading while out here would be acceptable to her ladyship."

Richard laughed. "One is never quite sure what will be acceptable to our dear Cathy. She is a young lady with definite opinions on almost everything."

"True. And, in all honesty, I would rather have that than a woman who sits about batting her eyelashes or thinking only about what new clothes are in fashion."

"Agreed. Catherine tends to keep us on our toes - not a bad thing at all. There you are, my friend. Sit here and keep an eye out for Mr. Getaway, while I go and make sure lunch will be served promptly when the aforementioned opinionated lady arrives. God forbid she should be kept waiting."

Chapter 6

Hawkesbury Manor, May 1587

Having made the pretext to Richard that he wished to stay up late reading and would get himself to bed, Jeremy sat quietly at his desk waiting for the house to settle down. He left the draperies ajar so John would know where to come.

The moon's fingers paved a golden road to the manor as they softly slipped through the small, newly-formed leaves of the oak trees lining the long drive. Her sparkling courtiers added their brilliance to a world dark only in the shadows cast by solid structures. All this light did not lend itself to the inconspicuous visit planned by John Hawkins. After passing through the gates at the road entrance, he dismounted and continued on foot.

He moved cautiously around the side of the house walking softly on the flagstone walk leading to the French doors through which a light cast a welcoming glow. John tapped on the glass and opened the door.

"John!" Jeremy said softly.

John hurried across the room to his brother and grasped him around the shoulders. "It has been a long time, little brother. You look like a man now, rather than the 18 year-old boy I left four years ago."

"I shall forgo saying you are looking like an old man now what with pointy beard, mustache and sunburned face." Jeremy's blue eyes sparkled as chuckled and continued, "Faith, but it's good to see you, John."

"And it's good to see you too. As to the whiskers and sunburn, if you had been sailing through the abominably hot climate which I had to endure, your pale skin would have been redder than sunset on a hot day. And would be devilishly painful." John drew a chair closer to Jeremy and sat down heavily. He sighed. "It's been a fair ride today."

"Then you must have something to quench your thirst," Jeremy said. "The supply is over there, as you know," he continued, nodding to the ornately carved credence cupboard. "Forgive me for not asking sooner."

As John helped himself to some wine, his eye fell on the wheeled bench. "What is that curiosity?"

"Something Richard dreamed up for me, probably right after you left. A great convenience. When I sit on it, he can push me around quite easily. Saves him doing a lot of carrying."

"Very clever. And how is Mrs. Owl?"

"Same as always - rather dour, but does her job and never complains ... at least not through speech - or screech." They both chuckled.

"And our darling baby sister?"

"Not so much of a baby anymore. In fact, she thinks she is quite old, or will be next year when she attains the great age of 18."

"Eighteen! I had imagined her still a gawky young girl. Then again, I guess Europe must have had some influence on her demeanor."

"Trust me. Our baby sister did not change a whit. She is as independent and talkative as ever."

"Really? Perhaps that's a good thing. It must have been hard for her growing up with no Mother, and having Father die so suddenly. "

"Would have been much harder for both of us if we hadn't had you, John. You were the best older brother, mother, father either of us could have asked for."

"All I can say is, I tried."

"I gather you did not come all this way in the middle of the night just to inquire after the family. And I must admit I am rather burning with curiosity."

"As I haven't much time, let me assuage your curiosity immediately. You are sure everyone is asleep?"

"Yes. It's after midnight, and all have been retired since 10 o'clock."

John pulled his chair closer. "As we speak, Francis Drake is on his way to Spain to attack the fleet of that odious Philip. In fact, he may already have arrived in Cadiz. I'm sure his mission will be quite successful. But Francis and I are quite as sure Philip, already seething with anger at Elizabeth's constant rejection of his marriage proposals, will not hesitate to retaliate in some way. How, exactly, we don't know. And that is why I've come to see you."

Jeremy looked quite puzzled. "I don't understand how that involves me."

"You can be of extreme help to us. We need someone who is loyal to Her Majesty, someone who is unafraid, and most of all, someone who can pretend to be something he is not. In short, a spy."

Jeremy frowned. "A spy. You mean a repeat of the Boar's Head?"

"Something like that, but not the Boar's Head, of course. Remember when we were young how you used to organize the four of us into little skits, at the acting of which you were always the best?"

"Yes, but ..."

"And we are aware you're afraid of nothing - not even the mean and angry bull who would have frightened a grown man, let alone a lad of twelve."

Jeremy shrugged. "I was just trying to protect Catherine. He would have killed her."

"And instead he trampled your legs and left a permanent reminder on your face."

Jeremy ran his finger over the silvery-purplish skin on his left jawline. "Better than a lost life. But you surely can't suggest I should be a spy in disguise! God above, I cannot even walk, as you mentioned! There is no way to disguise that."

"And that's why you would be absolutely the right person."

"You are mad!"

"Not at all. We have a perfect plan. All we need to implement it is you."

"Perhaps you'd best explain this perfect plan." Jeremy stared at his brother.

"I shall. But I need you to agree to accept the mission before I tell you what the plan is. Let me warn you though. The job is not without danger. You will have to be very, very careful. The numbers of those who hate Elizabeth and would love to see Philip crush England under his heel, are quite large. And Philip, of course, is quite willing to pay these traitors to help him. You will have to leave Hawkesbury Manor for an indeterminate amount of time - that is to say, until we have an opportunity to decimate Philip once and for all. This may be of a much longer duration than your few months at The Boar's Head, or it may be shorter. We don't know for sure."

Jeremy clasped his fingers and sat without speaking as his mind rapidly mulled over what his John had said.

John sipped his wine and watched his brother.

Several minutes passed during which the only sound was the chirping of a cricket from its spot on the hearth. Finally, Jeremy broke the silence. "I'll do it."

John clapped his brother's shoulder. "I knew we could count on you," he said happily.

"So tell me what I must do."

"There is a tavern situated on the Thames in the village of Tiddlebury not far from London. Thanks to the good graces of the innkeeper, a very loyal servant of the Queen, we have become aware certain personages who frequent his premises will do anything for money, even turn traitor to their country and Queen. It seems the Spanish spies prefer a bit nicer place than an alehouse when they're making contact with the English traitors. Ian McIntosh, the owner, has agreed to have you come and stay at the Crown & Anchor indefinitely until you come into some kind of information which will allow us to deal a fatal blow to Philip's plans, whatever they may be."

"If you are right about the caliber of people who frequent this inn, surely I will stick out like a sore thumb and people will become suspicious - especially those who are on the lookout for enemies."

"Very true, my dear brother, but I'm sure I can count on your fertile imagination to make sure you don't 'stick out.'"

"Aaah. I see." Jeremy smiled. "This is where the disguise comes in." He nodded. "I shall not disappoint."

"Make no mistake. This is not a lark and I must reiterate - you will be in a very dangerous position. One slip could give it all away and I shudder to think what might happen to you."

"I understand. Is the innkeeper aware of my reason for coming there?"

"No. Francis and I trust no one. Ian McIntosh knows only you are a friend of my valet and are coming there to write a book. But he is a good man and will assist you in every way possible. Oh!" John reached into his pocket. "The Queen herself asked we give you this in appreciation for your service. She said - now let me make sure I remember what Francis told me - yes, Her Majesty said, "Tell him if he should ever need assistance from us, send me this ring by messenger." John handed him a small velvet bag.

When Jeremy removed the ring, his breath was taken away as he stared at the sparkling red ruby. "This must be worth a fortune. And I'm to send the ring to her if I need help of some sort?"

"Right, and if it turns out you don't use the ring for that purpose, you are to keep it for helping."

"Keep it?!"

"Yes. Her Majesty wanted to let you know she's very appreciative of your past efforts."

"Most kind and generous of her, I'm sure." Jeremy slipped the ring on his left finger. "How much time do I have to get ready?"

"We'd like you there as soon as possible but we realize you must have things to do before leaving here. Say, five weeks? And I'm not sure wearing the ring is a good idea. Might raise too many questions."

"You're right, of course," Jeremy said, replacing the ring in the velvet bag and putting it in a small desk drawer. "You can expect to find me in place by the beginning of July."

"Most excellent."

Jeremy chewed his lip and frowned as he looked off into space.

"You look a little puzzled, Jeremy. Have I been unclear about something?"

"No, no. Not at all. I just remembered something rather odd."

"What's that?"

"David Lancaster came to see me a few months back and said he thought I might be requested by you to get involved in something or other, although he wasn't sure what."

"Really? Hmmm. I wonder where he got his information."

"I have no idea. The odd part was he asked me not to get involved."

"Strange. You should have told me before I explained the plan to you."

"Why? David is an old friend and has spied for the Queen on many occasions."

"I know. But we are somewhat concerned over him as his visits to Spain have increased dramatically over the last couple of years and he hasn't returned for several months. Our contact lost track of him. Too much drinking at our expense, I suspect!"

"Oh." Jeremy laughed. "Is that what bothers you? Fear not. David has fallen in love with the most wonderful woman in the world, if you can believe what he says. They plan to be married, and he is going to live in Spain - in fact, by what you say, he may be married already."

"I see. That would certainly explain why he has been travelling back and forth so much and why he hasn't been seen recently. However, we had no intention of using him as your contact this time anyway, just to be on the safe side."

"Who will take his place?"

"No one. We will use a different way. There is an illiterate stable boy named Adam who is employed by the inn. He will be able to deliver messages to my valet, as long as you give him explicit directions to my house. He is swift of foot, not of mind. And despite being close, you must never come to see me, nor will I see you."

"I understand. And your valet's name?"

"Anthony Turner."

"Good. Young Adam can be my feet."

"Indeed. Now, I must leave, Jeremy. I need to be on the road before first light. It would not do well for anyone to know I have been here." John came to his brother, leaned down and put his arms around him. "You are a brave man, Jemmy, which is why I knew we could count on you." John straightened up and shook Jeremy's hand. "God bless you in your mission."

"Thank you, John. Godspeed."

John disappeared as quietly as he had arrived.

Chapter 7

Hawkesbury Manor, May 1587

Tired though he was, Jeremy had trouble falling asleep as he kept mulling over how he could implement the perfect disguise. He realized being crippled would be an enormous asset, as his experience over the years had been that upon meeting him, people assumed, for a reason which he could never fathom, being unable to walk also meant he was dim-witted. Invariably, this led to them speaking slowly and loudly a few inches from his face, until he informed them, without rancour, he was neither deaf nor dumb. This time, he decided, he would add stuttering to reinforce people's assumption. Eventually, he dozed off into a land where unsettling dreams spoke of fear and suffering.

He was abruptly aroused from the arms of Morpheus by the noise of drapes being flung back to admit the early morning light, followed by Catherine calling him.

"Wake up sleepyhead! It's a beautiful morning." She came to his bedside and pulled the bed curtains aside. "The sun is shining and I'm going out for a ride. I'll be back in half an hour and I expect to find you sitting at the breakfast table ready to enjoy Mrs. Stewart's famous toad-in-the-hole."

"I don't know how famous her toad-in-the-hole is, but I do know you're famous for raising the dead at some ungodly hour of the morning. Go away!"

"I shan't leave until you promise to get out of bed."

"No!"

"I will start singing," she said in a warning tone.

"Oh no! Not that," Jeremy feigned dismay. "Anything but your singing."

"Oh yes I will, you know."

"Much to my sorrow, I do know." Jeremy groaned. "All right, you win. I'll get up."

Catherine leaned over and kissed his forehead. "Good boy. Breakfast will be on the table in half an hour. Now I'm off." She hurried out the glass doors.

Jeremy lay there for a few seconds.

Catherine peeked back around the door, her hair a blazing halo around her face. "I don't see you moving. Do I have to sing?"

"No! Go away, you terrible girl! I am getting up. Leave!"

Her laughter faded away as she hurried down the path.

Jeremy was through his morning ablutions and dressed by the time Richard came to take him to the breakfast room.

"I was informed by her ladyship you would be ready and waiting for me by now," Richard said, smiling.

"Catherine doesn't leave one much choice when she wants something done."

The breakfast room was bright and cheery thanks to the tapestries, whose brilliant threads were brought to life by the sunlight streaming in the window. Hyacinths and lily-of-the valley lining the walkway leading to the beautiful gardens at the back of the house were framed by the doorway. Delicious smells emanated from the several serving bowls arranged in the centre of the highly polished oak table.

As promised, both young men were at the breakfast table when Catherine returned.

"Did you enjoy your ride?" Jeremy asked.

"Indeed. It would have been better if I hadn't been waylaid by Lord Piggy's piglet son, William."

"Catherine, you shouldn't call the Earl of Fotheringham that," Jeremy admonished her. "He can't help what he looks like." Four miles away, the Earl and Countess of Fotheringham were their nearest neighbours.

"I know, but he has a nose that looks like it was squashed by a melon and shoved up into those tiny pig eyes that peer at you, as if he's afraid he might be trussed up on a spit at any moment. Anyway, William insisted on riding along with me for a short distance." She rolled her eyes. "He rides so slowly. Although come to think of it, that's not entirely a bad thing because I was able to escape by challenging him to a race and, of course, left him six furlongs behind." Catherine laughed.

"I suppose there is no point in asking you not to ride so fast, Catherine?" Jeremy said.

"Good. Then you won't ask, will you?" she said, helping herself to more syrup. "I did find out something interesting from him though. He told me his sister, Jenny, was being sent to France for a year, to improve her manners or something silly like that." She looked at Richard. "I hope you aren't too upset, Richard," she said slyly.

"Why in the world would I be upset?" Richard asked.

"Because she's sweet on you, of course. Now here she is taking off for Paris where all those lecherous Frenchmen live. While I was there, I heard they all have at least one mistress even though they're married and they don't hesitate to kiss or hug any woman they please."

"I thought you were in school. Wherever did you get this questionable information?" Jeremy asked.

"One hears things," she replied obliquely. "Italians are not much better, of course, although I was able to put them in their place. And did you know Italian courtesans wear ruffled things called bloomers, sort of like men's breeches, but prettier, of course? Actually, I think they would be a good idea for ladies to wear when riding. Then I wouldn't have so much trouble trying to get my leg over Starlight's back."

"Really, Catherine! There are some things ladies do not discuss," Jeremy said reprovingly, "and under-garments are one of them."

"Oh. So ladies can't discuss their own clothes but men can?" she replied.

"That's not what I said."

"That's what you meant. Anyway, I've said it. Please pass the butter."

Jeremy shook his head and sighed.

Richard cleared his throat. "And where do you get the idea I care whether or not Jenny Harrison goes to France or that she's 'sweet' on me?"

"I thought you were probably enamored of her, Richard. How could you possibly not see those big brown eyes following your every step at the fayre last Christmas? Surely those love beams pierced your heart and made you fall in love with her."

Jeremy nearly choked on a sausage trying not to laugh.

"What nonsense you speak! Love beams piercing my heart indeed! I am not now, nor have I ever been 'enamored' of Miss Harrison," he replied firmly. "You can get that silly notion out of your head."

"Humph! Another thing. The rest of the family is going to Sheffield to attend the death of an aunt - Mrs. Harrison's sister, I think she is."

"That's too bad. I hope you expressed our condolences."

"Certainly I did, Jemmy. I am not without manners, you know. Of course, I didn't mention you would say the poor woman would be coming back to life some time in the future. They would have thought me a witch." She paused. "Hmmm. Maybe I should have. I could just imagine William's eyes popping out at that piece of information."

"I realize not everyone believes in reincarnation, Cathy, but there is much information on the subject - enough to make me firmly believe we do come back several times over. You should read some of the books I have about it."

"Well, if I do have to come back from wherever I am, I want to be a man with oodles of money so I can travel and see the world."

"Would you really like to do that, Catherine? See the world, I mean?" Richard asked, with some excitement in his voice.

"Certainly. Who wouldn't? Imagine what wonderful adventures one could have."

Richard smiled. "I agree. Sounds like a splendid idea to me."

Jeremy regarded Catherine. "You might be interested to know the same people often reincarnate with each other, sometimes for a particular reason. It's possible we lived together before."

"I'm sure if we lived together before, I'd remember."

"Not necessarily, although some people have flashes of memories."

"What particular reason could anyone have for wanting to come back with the same people?" Catherine asked.

"Oh, different things. Some kind of unfinished business perhaps. Maybe lovers want to come back to be with each other again."

"Really? That would be very romantic. Imagine! Love survives death and lives forever." Catherine sighed. "I wonder if that could happen to me."

"You never know. It might, assuming you ever find anyone who is willing to put up with you." Jeremy laughed.

"Well! Are you implying no one will ever fall in love with me? How horrid of you!" she said indignantly. "Not that I give a fig if they do or not," she said, tilting her chin skywards. "I have you and Richard and it's most certainly a fact the two of you are more trouble than you're worth. Why would I want to have another man tramping about?!"

The young men burst out laughing.

"See? You're horrible - both of you!" Catherine said, as she stuffed another forkful of food in her mouth.

They continued eating in silence for a few minutes.

"In fact, Catherine, I hope you will find someone who loves you dearly and will take care of you." Jeremy said. "I may not always be here."

Catherine and Richard stared at Jeremy. "Oh, don't look upset. I'm not talking about dying, although we're all going to do that some day. What I'm referring to is leaving here for a while."

"What? Why? Where are you going? Why would you want to leave here?" Catherine said, dropping her fork on her plate.

Jeremy had spent a good portion of the night devising a plausible story of why he would be leaving and where he would be going. It remained for him to make his story sound convincing. "You know I am much interested in various ancient traditions involving rituals, practices and beliefs, such as reincarnation, which we were just mentioning. I sent a letter to the relatively new university in Edinburgh, giving my credentials and asking if they would be offering a course which might be of interest to me. It turns out they are indeed, and I have been accepted into the program."

The two listeners appeared stunned. Finally, Catherine exclaimed, "Scotland??! You are going all the way to Scotland?"

"I am indeed. Didn't you just tell me the other day I should have some adventures? I think this will be one, don't you agree?"

"I think it's a splendid idea, Jemmy. I'm sure you'll enjoy yourself immensely. And you can rest assured I will take very good care of Catherine ... I mean everything here, including Miss Catherine," Richard said, rising and coming to Jeremy. "Congratulations, my friend." They shook hands.

"I know I can trust you to see to the running of Hawkesbury Manor, Richard. I will rest easy knowing things are in your capable hands. Thank you."

"Can't you take me with you?"

"You would be bored before the first day ended, Catherine. I will be busy with classes, assignments and endless reading. Wish me well."

Catherine's pout turned to a smile. "It's a shock, but indeed you should go and have a marvellous time," Catherine said, regaining her good spirits. She hugged her brother. "When are you leaving?"

"Somewhere near the end of June. There is much to be done before I leave. I am going to ask Aunt Annabelle to come and stay here while I'm gone. And your cousin Mary, of course. She will be fine company for you."

"MARY?! That silly girl who's afraid of her own shadow? Who doesn't even know how to ride a horse? THAT Mary??"

"Maybe she's learned to ride a horse since the last time you saw her, and if she hasn't, perhaps you could teach her how. Maybe she's changed."

Catherine looked at him balefully. "And maybe elephants will grow wings and fly," she said.

"Cheer up, Cathy. It won't be that bad. I'm sure you will have some fun together, and I shall be content knowing you will have some female company while I'm gone. I know you like Aunt Annabelle."

Catherine rolled her eyes. "Some things in life are soooo ... soooo ...." Her voice trailed off.

"I can't believe it! Our dear Cathy is stuck for a word. Wonders will never cease," Jeremy said.

Catherine stuck out her tongue at him and marched out of the room, leaving the two young men laughing aloud.

Chapter 8

Hawkesbury Manor, June 1587

As part of his disguise, Jeremy decided to grow a beard, and by the time Annabelle and Mary Ainsworth arrived, his month's growth was quite substantial. Catherine had plenty to say about him not shaving. When her remark that the beard made him look like an old man seemed to please Jeremy, she resigned herself to his hirsute appearance and commented further that some men didn't have the sense of a fly.

Richard and two servants hastened outside to assist the Ainsworth ladies out of their coach and bring in their luggage. Mrs. Pedley conducted them to their rooms and left after advising refreshments would be ready for them whenever they chose to come downstairs where Jeremy was waiting to receive them in the drawing-room. To no one's surprise, Cathy had disappeared, despite Jeremy's admonition she was to behave and be on hand to welcome their guests.

Breathing heavily, Annabelle Ainsworth entered the drawing-room, her short neck popping up from an extremely large ruff that encircled her shoulders, making her look like a prehistoric reptile. Frizzy, red hair was piled high on her head and topped off with a spangled-covered caul. Despite the warmth of May, she wore a long-sleeved black velvet dress, heavily embroidered on either side of the skirt, which featured a panel of gold brocade running from the high neck down to the floor.

Mary followed behind her mother, in a dark green dress with a v-shaped insert starting at the shoulders and ending at the waistline. Her ruff, although much narrower, was no less elaborate than her mother's. As befitted a young, unmarried girl, Mary's waist-length, chestnut brown hair cascaded loosely over the ruff, and past her ample bosom, modestly hidden despite the square neckline of her dress. The back of her head, featured a caul similar in style to her mother's.

"Aunt Annabelle! How wonderful to see you," Jeremy said. "And Mary! What a beautiful young lady you have become."

Annabelle kissed Jeremy briefly on the cheek before collapsing into a nearby chair and commencing to fan her face. Droplets of perspiration left paler rivulets down her whitened face, and the chair quivered with each frantic motion of her arm.

Mary smiled and seated herself opposite her mother. "Where's Catherine?"

"Out riding, I believe. She should be here very shortly though. I know she's looking forward to seeing you."

"How nice," Mary said, in a voice which indicated she would more likely believe the house was about to fall down around their heads than her cousin would be glad to see her.

"How was your trip?"

"La," Annabelle began, "it was beastly, what with this unseasonably warm weather and uncomfortably hard seats in the coach. It's very hard on one's fragile constitution. But one mustn't complain. Other poor souls have to walk, which my delicate feet just could not possibly do."

"Sorry I'm late," Catherine said, coming across the room. "How are you, Aunt Annabelle?"

Annabelle looked aghast at Catherine. "Whatever are you doing in that peasant's garb, child? And your face? So ... so ... "

"Normal-looking?" Catherine finished. "I have no intention of EVER painting my face with ghastly white paint. It makes women look like ghosts called from their graves by Druids on Samhain."

"Oh, la!" Annabelle slapped her hand on her chest in the region of her heart. The fan moved faster and the chair quivered more than before. "I think I'm going to faint."

"As to my clothes," Catherine continued, "how in the world would I ever get on a horse if I were wearing one of those big hoops? My skirts would be up over my head for all the world to see my undergarments and who knows what else."

Mary tittered.

"Mercy!" Annabelle's fan moved vigorously. The chair threatened to collapse.

"Catherine!" Jeremy remonstrated. "Apologize to your aunt right now."

"I'm sorry if I've offended you, Aunt Annabelle, but I only speak the truth. As I told Jemmy a while back, Italian courtesans wear ruffled bloomers and if I ..."

"Cathy! Why don't you give some lemonade to your aunt and cousin?"

"Of course." Catherine poured the cool drink into crystal glasses. As she handed one to her aunt, she lifted a portion of her aunt's velvet skirt. "La, Aunty, it's no wonder you're hot. This material is so heavy, you must be sweating to death!"

"Ladies do not sweat, Catherine, although perhaps you're not aware of this?" said Mary sweetly.

Catherine laughed. "Fiddlesticks! Just one of the many fallacies invented by women to dupe men into thinking they are delicate creatures with some weird kind of body that doesn't do the same sort of things as men and animals, except pigs who do not sweat, unlike humans who all sweat."

"Cathy, I'm sure you can find something to talk about other than the peculiarities of human and animal functions," Jeremy said.

Catherine looked to the ceiling for inspiration. "What have you been doing, Mary? Have you learned to ride a horse? I hope so. I can take you on a perfectly lovely ride if you have."

"Certainly I can ride a horse. I had a private instructor who taught me how to ride like a lady. "

Cathy rolled her eyes. "Good. Then perhaps tomorrow we can ride together."

"Catherine, why don't you take Mary out to view the gardens? I'm sure it will be quite pleasant in the summerhouse, and you could take your lemonade there."

"Sounds like a good idea. Come along, Mary," Catherine said, heading toward the door.

Somewhat reluctantly, Mary followed.

"Wait!" Jeremy called out to the girls. "Do you care to join them, Aunt Isabelle?"

"No thank you, Jeremy. In fact, I think I would like to go lie down for a while, if you don't mind."

"I quite understand. Would you like any assistance from Mrs. Pedley? I've no doubt she has a maid who would be available to you"

"How very thoughtful of you, Jeremy. I would indeed like that." The chair gave an audible sigh when Annabelle stood.

"Catherine ..."

"I'll send Mrs. Pedley in," Cathy said. "Come along, Mary. Mrs. P. is likely in the kitchen."

"Can't you just ring for her?" Mary said.

"Why ring a bell when we have perfectly good legs to take us to the kitchen?"

"I don't understand why you should go looking for servants. They are supposed to come when they're called."

Catherine laughed. "Oooh, I'd love to see Mrs. Pedley's face if she heard you call her a servant. She may not think she's one of the family, but she certainly doesn't regard herself as a servant!"

The girls entered the kitchen and Catherine inhaled deeply. "It smells WONDERFUL in here, Mrs. Stewart. Are you making some of your scrumptious caramel pudding?"

"I am that, Miss Catherine, but ye'll be getting none till dinnertime."

"How naughty of you to make me wait! But I do think you're very brave to be cooking in all this heat." Catherine gave the rosy-cheeked cook a hug. "You remember my cousin, Mary."

"Very pleased to have you stay with us, Miss, I'm sure." Mrs. Stewart bobbed quickly.

Mary nodded.

"And I'm sure you must have some other delicious goody around we can have now," said Catherine.

"Away with ye, tryin' to wheedle an old woman like meself with flattery," Mrs. Stewart smiled broadly. "There just might be a slice or two of lemon bread in the pantry."

"I knew it! That will go very nicely with our lemonade. Thank you, Mrs. Stewart. Oh, there you are, Mrs. Pedley. Would you be so kind as to go and fetch my auntie and take her upstairs to her rooms. She's with Jeremy now."

Mrs. Pedley nodded and disappeared down the hallway.

Catherine retrieved the bread and the girls went out into the garden.

"This way," she said. "You may remember Mr. Getaway, our resident fish in the pond, but I don't think you'll see him. He tends to hide, especially during the day. But if you do want to look, don't go too close. You might frighten him."

"I wouldn't go looking for Mr. Getaway or any other fish. They stink." Mary wrinkled her nose.

"There's the summerhouse. Isn't it lovely? Jemmy had Richard build it while I was away. We can have our lemonade in there."

The girls passed between two huge stones which sat one on each side of a small bridge over the channel surrounding the summerhouse.

"Very nice." Mary sat down on the bench. "You are so lucky to have visited France and Italy. What's it like in Paris?"

"Well, there are scads of old buildings and churches. It seems like bells are ringing from morning to night. A great many people too, especially artists. I mean they aren't ringing bells, but they do line the banks of the river."

"But what about fashions? What are the ladies wearing?"

"Clothes, of course. The same as here."

"Surely there must be something new."

"Not that I noticed."

"How disappointing. Well, what about the men?"

"What do you mean? Their clothes are about the same as here and they don't look any different from any other men, except maybe there are more mustaches."

Mary rolled her eyes. "I mean how do they act toward women? I heard they are very romantic, and so ... daring."

"Oh that. In France there is much hand-kissing if they think they can get away with it, and I was told all the men have at least one mistress, even if they have a wife. In Rome, they are always trying to touch you, even perfect strangers, and try to be very charming, like the French men. They have mistresses too."

"How delicious! I wish I could go to Paris or Rome."

Catherine looked incredulous. "Because of the men? You want to be a mistress!? What a silly notion."

"Not a mistress, exactly - that is ridiculous. I am grown up now and I need a man to be my lover and make me a complete woman."

"A complete woman? Are you missing some parts?"

"Of course I'm not missing any parts, but I have parts that haven't bloomed yet. I want to experience ... everything. If you know what I mean." Mary raised her eyebrows, tilted her head and looked sideways at Catherine.

"Oh. That."

"Exactly. And I want a husband eventually, but in the meantime ..." Mary patted her hair. "Do you have a gentleman friend? Someone special?"

"No. And I don't want anyone."

"Now you are being silly. Or maybe you're too young. Father is very tedious and won't hold any receptions for me until I turn 18, even though there are several eligible young men who are dying to pay court to me. I can tell from their glances. And if by any chance, they can spend a few moments alone with me, they virtually fall at my feet. Nothing happens though because someone is always around." Mary sighed.

"Hmph! I'd rather have adventures."

"Adventures? Like what?"

"Oh I don't know. Maybe travel somewhere far away. Discover some place new like Jacques Cartier did ... the wilds of a new continent." Catherine looked dreamily into space.

"I have no wish to go anywhere else, unless to meet handsome young men. Are there any around here?"

"Any what?"

"Men. Are there any young men here? I want to meet some handsome, dashing man who will take me in his arms and make love to me. Do you know one?"

"A handsome young man." Catherine thought for a moment. Mischief filled her eyes and a laugh threatened to explode from her mouth. "Why yes, we will probably meet one when we go riding."

"Really? Wonderful! What's his name?"

"William Harrison. His family lives a little distance from us."

"How do you know we'll meet him if we go riding?"

"Because he always waits for me by the stream where we water the horses. You are very beautiful, Mary, and I know he will fall in love with you immediately."

"How wonderful! When are we going to go?"

"Tomorrow morning."

"I can hardly wait."

Mary didn't notice Catherine's impish smile.

Chapter 9

Hawkesbury Manor, June 1587

Catherine knocked loudly on her cousin's bedroom door.

"Mary!" She waited, knocked again. "Mary! Are you awake?" Catherine called loudly. "Time to get up! We are to go riding this morning, remember?"

The door opened slowly and Mary peered at her cousin through half-closed lids. "What time is it? Surely terribly early."

"Nearly eight o'clock. You said you wanted to go riding this morning, so time to get moving."

"By morning, I meant an hour before noon. Mother says ladies do not appear in public until at least 11 o'clock."

"What nonsense! I have been appearing every day well before that time. Hurry up and get dressed. My poor Lightning will be wondering where I am. I'll have them saddle up Star for you. Quickly now. The lovely day awaits. I'll be at the stables when you come."

Catherine dashed off down the stairs and stopped to check her brother's room. Jeremy was seated at his desk apparently making a list of something.

"Good morning, Jemmy." Catherine said, coming to him and kissing him on the forehead. "What's that?" she said, indicating the paper.

"A list of things I must remember to do before I leave."

"Oh don't talk about leaving. It makes me sad." She pulled his beard. "Especially when I know you'll be gone for so long."

"I'll be back before you realize I'm gone."

"It's going to seem like forever, what with tedious Mary being here. Can you believe she was still asleep when I knocked on her door a few minutes ago? Good heavens! What does a person need all that sleep for? There are so many more interesting things to do. I did get her up and moving - at least I hope she's moving. We are to go riding this morning, and I know Lightning will be getting restless wondering where I am. He is very used to me being there by now and bringing his treat." She frowned. "Oh bother! I had better get a treat for Mary to give Star." Catherine turned on her heel and headed quickly out the door.

Jeremy watched the whirlwind leave and smiled to himself before looking once more at his list of things to do. He had solved the clothes problem by asking Richard to find him some common-looking outfits, explaining he did not want to appear be a wealthy gentleman on the trip should his coach be accosted by a robber. Richard agreed. Jemmy planned on doing his own packing at night, including a few of his good clothes, to avoid any questions. A couple of his favourite books would also be making the trip.

His mind turned back to Catherine and he chuckled to himself as he thought of the merry chase she would likely lead Mary over whatever length of time she and Annabelle remained here.

The sister of whom he was thinking was at that moment in the stables mulling over how she would entertain her cousin, or, more accurately, how she would be able to foist her off on someone else. Absentmindedly, she patted Lightning's head.

"Oh well. Something is likely to occur to me. I'm not usually without ideas. Maybe she'll actually like William."

"Pardon me, Miss?" said Donald. The young man in charge of the stable stood up after tightening the saddle straps.

"Nothing, Donald. I was talking to myself."

"Very good, miss. Horses are ready to go. Is the other young lady coming shortly?"

"I think so."

"Good, because Star is getting restless, wanting to get going."

"Lead them outside, Donald. We'll wait there."

"Very good, Miss."

Mary arrived a few minutes later and found Donald waiting to assist her. Her breath caught and she looked appraisingly at the tall young man. His dark hair fell forward over his face as he bent down and cupped his hand to assist her onto the saddle.

"How very kind of you," Mary said, smiling as she gazed directly into his brown eyes. "What is your name?"

"Donald. At your service, Miss."

"Thank you, Donald." Mary pressed her hand into his as she took the reins.

His eyebrows raised as he smiled and withdrew his hand. "It was my pleasure, Miss."

"Not entirely," Mary said to herself as she turned her horse around.

"Whatever is keeping you?" Catherine called impatiently.

"Coming," Mary replied.

"Finally!"

"Donald is very handsome, isn't he?" Mary said, smiling as she looked back and discovered he was still watching them.

"I suppose so. I hadn't thought about it."

"I realize he's just hired help, but how could you not think about his beautiful eyes?"

"Because I have better things to think about," Catherine said, giving her horse a slap on the flank.

The girls headed out across the meadow with Catherine setting the pace at a quick walk. She turned Lightning into the woods, following a path they both knew well where the bright morning sunlight played hide and seek through the leaves. Forest creatures scurried out of their way and birds momentarily ceased their song.

The path eventually led them to a clearing through which a stream gurgled over rocks. Catherine pulled up.

"Isn't this beautiful?" she said, drawing in a deep breath. "My very favourite spot in the whole world. At least until I visit some new and exotic land." She slid off her horse, and Lightning made for the stream.

Mary looked around. "How am I supposed to get down?"

Catherine looked confused. "Like I did, of course. Slide off."

"I can't do that. I might break an ankle. Someone usually helps me down."

Catherine rolled her eyes, and turned at the sound of horse's hooves.

"Looks like someone is coming to your rescue, cousin." Catherine sat on a large rock to watch.

William Harrison rode into the clearing as Star, growing impatient waiting for her rider to dismount, headed for the stream.

"Stop! Stop, you beast! I shall fall off!"

William dismounted quickly, ran to Star and stopped her progression.

"Settle, girl. Settle." He looked up at Mary. "Are you wanting to get off, Miss?"

Mary looked at Catherine who obviously did not intend to help. "Indeed. If you would be so kind," she said, reluctantly extending her arms.

"It would be my pleasure," William said. His face flushed as he put his arms on her waist and lifted her down.`

Mary eyed him as she did all members of the opposite sex. He was not as tall as Donald, but still a few inches over her head. She decided his short nose, small mouth and close-set eyes gave him the appearance of being a relative of Mr. Getaway who somehow was managing to live outside the pond. She drew back quickly.

Catherine saw Mary's reaction and turned away to hide her smile.

"You must be a friend of Catherine's," he said. "I'm William. William Harrison, but please call me Will."

"As you wish."

William nervously ran his fingers through his ash blond hair.

"This is my cousin, Mary Ainsworth," Catherine said. "Quite beautiful, is she not?"

Mary did not look happy.

"Oh." Will realized he had forgotten about Catherine. "Hello, Cathy."

Catherine rolled her eyes as she bent over and ran her hand through the water.

"Miss Ainsworth, would you care to sit down here?" Will said, indicating a large, platform-like stone, big enough to seat two comfortably. He removed his jacket and laid it down.

"I think I would prefer to sit over here," Mary said, as she moved toward her cousin.

William rushed over and placed his jacket on the empty spot to the right of Catherine. After Mary had settled herself, he sat on the ground close to her feet. Mary glared at Catherine who was staring fixedly at the water on her left.

William squirmed a little and cleared his throat. "How long have you been here, Miss, or more importantly, how long are you staying?"

"I'm not sure." Mary looked up at the trees.

"Jemmy's going away and Mary's going to stay awhile. Quite a long while, most likely. You're sure to see her often, right Mary?" Catherine said, smiling innocently.

Mary glowered at her cousin.

William did not take his eyes off Mary. "So where do you live?"

"Not far from London."

"My family went to London a long time ago. Do you have brothers and sisters?"

"No." Mary said sharply. "All these questions are boring."

William's pale face turned a bright red and he bit his thin bottom lip. "Oh, I do apologize. I didn't mean ..." His voice trailed off.

"Shall we ride on now?" Mary said.

"Already? But I thought we were having a good time visiting." Catherine picked up a stone and tossed it across the water.

"Oh yes. Please stay a while longer," William said.

"I'd rather go. We haven't had breakfast yet and I feel a little faint. I'd like to go back."

Cathy stood. "Oh, all right. I think the horses have had enough to eat and drink, so I guess we can ride on." She whistled to Lightning.

William rose with alacrity and offered his hand to Mary. She ignored his gesture, but quickly realized she would need help mounting Star. "Thank you," she said stiffly, taking his hand.

"You're most welcome, I'm sure." William walked with her to Star's side and cupped his hands. "I hope it's nothing serious."

"What?"

"Your illness."

Mary rolled her eyes. The man was an idiot. "I'll be fine." She finished the sentence in her head. *As soon as I get away from you.'*

Catherine was already starting to move off. "Come on, slow-pokes." Seeing the other two mounted, she spurred her horse forward and crossed the clearing.

"Wait!" Mary yelled.

Catherine was fast getting out of earshot.

"It's no use," William said. "That mare isn't called Lightning for nothing. But don't worry, I'll see you get home safely."

Mary pursed her lips and frowned. "Surely Catherine will wait ahead somewhere," she said, urging her horse forward.

"Let's not worry about Catherine and just enjoy a pleasant ride," William said.

Mary looked at him scornfully, but didn't express what she was thinking, knowing she was going to need his help in finding Hawkins Manor. Neither rider noticed Catherine had circled around and was following at a distance.

When Mary caught a glimpse of the manor house in the distance, she reined in. "I can see where I am now. It is not necessary for you to come any further."

"I would be happy to escort you right to the stables, Miss Ainsworth. I don't mind."

The word "stables" brought up an image of a handsome young man. "That's not necessary," Mary said firmly. "I will be quite fine."

"Oh." William was clearly disappointed. "I hope we will meet again tomorrow ... or whenever you go riding again."

Mary ignored his remark and headed for the manor as fast as she dared to ride. When she reached the stables, a young lad of twelve or so came hurrying out and took hold of Star's bridle.

"Oh. Who are you?"

"Robert, but they call me Bobby, Miss."

"Where's Donald?"

Bobby nodded toward the stable. "Inside, Miss, tending to a horse."

"Please tell him I require his services."

"Yes, Miss."

Bobby disappeared through the door. Donald came out shortly.

"How can I help you, Miss?" he said.

Mary smiled and said in a frightened voice, "Would you assist me down, Donald? I didn't quite trust myself to the young boy."

"Certainly, Miss." Donald lifted her with ease, settled her on the ground and dropped his arms.

Mary held onto his shoulders. "Thank you. And you may call me Mary."

"If you say so, Miss."

"Mary."

"Miss Mary." Donald looked closely at Mary, still deciding whether he was interpreting her actions correctly. When girls in the village eyed him as she had, it meant they wanted more than a smile. However, this young woman was well above his class and a visitor to the manor. A little caution might be in order, he thought.

At that moment, Catherine came riding in.

"It was rather horrid of you to ride off and leave me," Mary said indignantly.

"You weren't alone and William knows his way here quite well. Besides, I was only a little distance off and watched you the whole way." She slid off her horse.

"Well why didn't you make your presence known?"

"I thought you and William were having a good time and I didn't want to spoil it."

Mary glared at her. "Hmpf! We were not." She looked pointedly at Donald. "I was definitely not happy in William's company."

"I'm not a mind-reader. How was I supposed to know? William certainly looked like he was enjoying your company, I think he's fallen madly in love with you."

Mary snorted.

Catherine turned her back to hide a smile. "Come along. It's nearly lunch time."

Mary hurried to keep up with Catherine's long stride. "How long has Donald been here?" she asked.

"I don't know for sure. Three years, I think."

"How old is he?"

"Ancient, I think. Probably about twenty-two. Why are you asking?"

"Just curious. I think he's very attractive."

"I suppose he is, if you like older men," Catherine said. "You aren't thinking of marrying him are you?"

"Of course not! He's only a stable hand. I shall marry some-one of nobility."

"Like William," Catherine said, smiling.

"Never in a million years," Mary said, entirely missing the fact Catherine had referred to William as being of the nobility.

Chapter 10

The Crown & Anchor, Tiddlebury, July 1587

After spending three days on the road, Jeremy was picked up early in the morning at the Tiddlebury station by Adam, the young lad mentioned to him by John. Adam was pleasant company and asked few questions, despite his curiosity about the crippled young man.

As they bounced along, Jeremy recalled the sight of Catherine, tears coursing down her cheeks, leaning against Richard's shoulder as she waved good-bye. Richard had his arm protectively around her and the thought had crossed Jeremy's mind they looked well-suited to each other, a notion which he had dismissed as quickly as it had come. The idea had barely surfaced again when it was chased away by their arrival at the Crown and Anchor.

"Here we are, sir." Following instructions, Adam drove the cart to the back of the inn and ran inside to announce the expected guest had arrived. In seconds, he was back to take hold of the horses' reins.

The man who followed him was as round as he was tall, with a grin that underlined his red nose and ruddy cheeks. To decide he was weak and out-of-shape because of his size, would be a big mistake. Muscles of iron bulged out below his rolled-up sleeves.

"Welcome! Welcome to the Crown & Anchor." He whisked Jeremy's meagre luggage off the cart and set it down on the ground. "Whist, Mrs. McIntosh," he said to the rotund woman who appeared at the door, "don't just stand there. Get some food on the table for the boy. You," he looked at Adam, "get yon bags in the house and mind you do a good job with they horses." Turning to Jeremy, he continued, "You must be Thomas Smithson. Ian McIntosh at your service, and very pleased we are to have you with us. Let me get you down off the cart."

Jeremy managed only one word, 'Thank', before the burly arms reached up, pulled him down and tossed him carefully over a broad shoulder.

"Where do you want this, sir?" Adam said, indicating the chair with wheels.

Ian looked with curiosity at the conveyance. "What is that?"

"It's something my good friend made for me so I could get around by myself without having to be carried all the time."

"Can't say I've ever seen anything like that," Ian said. "Well, don't stand there, boy. Take the chair inside with the rest of his things. Put it in the kitchen. And mind it isn't in Mrs. McIntosh's way."

"Yes sir." Adam hurried inside, followed by Ian and Jeremy.

As they went through the door, delicious smells of baking bread and cooking meat floated through the air, resulting in a rumble from Jeremy's stomach, a subtle reminder he had not eaten since the previous evening. Ian turned right into the kitchen and deposited Jeremy in a chair set by a table facing a fireplace where Mrs. McIntosh was ladling what looked like soup from a large pot hanging from an iron handle. She brought the bowl over to him, along with a thick slice of bread.

"It s-s-s-smells wonderful in h-here, M-M-Mrs. McIntosh."

"Oh you're going to love her cooking," Ian said. "That's why I married her. It's what keeps me healthy, although she doesn't feed me enough." He laughed as he patted his large belly.

"If ye were any bigger, Mr. McIntosh, ye'd never fit through the door. Here you are, Mr. Smithson."

"Thank you. P-please call me Thomas."

"We've got you a nice room down the hall to the right," he said, nodding his head back toward the door they had entered. "Mrs.

McIntosh and I have a room upstairs, but we thought you'd be better suited here. The room's got a window looking into our little garden. Mrs. McIntosh likes to grow some herbs, but it's Meggie what does the flowers." Pride filled his voice as he continued. "Meggie's our daughter. She helps out in the tavern."

"And a good thing she does, Mr. McIntosh, because for sure you'd never be able to run between the tables," Nancy McIntosh said, smiling at her husband.

"Whist! I would have nae trouble at all. It's just I'm too busy filling the tankards. Besides, folks would rather have a pretty girl wait on them rather than an old codger like me."

"Ye'll get no argument from me, Mr. McIntosh."

"Where is the girl anyway?"

"Right behind you, Father," said a tall young woman from the doorway.

"Come in and meet our new guest, Thomas Smithson. Mr. Smithson, our daughter, Meggie," Ian said, smiling broadly.

At the swish of skirts to his right, Jemmy looked up into the bright green eyes and smiling face of the loveliest woman he had ever seen. His mouth fell slightly open as he automatically took her extended hand.

At that moment, Jemmy was not a spy, not a scholar, not even a cripple. He was the man who, upon looking at a certain woman for the first time, falls immediately and hopelessly in love. He continued holding her hand until Meggie laughed.

"Cat got your tongue, Mr. Smithson?" she said.

Jeremy's face flushed and he released her hand quickly. "S-sorry. I'm very pleased to meet you, Miss McIntosh."

"There's no need to be so formal," Ian said. "Meggie is Meggie, Mrs. McIntosh is Nancy and I'm Ian."

Jeremy watched as Meggie took a seat opposite him. "There weren't too many weeds in your garden, Mommy. Everything is growing nicely."

"Good. Thank you, Meggie."

"So how long are you here for, Thomas?"

"I'm n-not sure. Probably a long t-time."

"Daddy tells me you're writing a book."

"Don't pester the young man, Meggie. He's got some eating to do and when he's finished I want to show him his room," Ian said.

"I don't mind, Ian. Yes, I'm writing a book and I'm hoping to get some local c-colour here."

"What's it about? People in small village who frequent the local tavern?"

Jeremy smiled. "Not quite, although I expect the villagers have many stories to tell, and I'm a good listener." Meggie looked at him expectantly. He continued, "Uh, well, the b-book has to do with life after death, different beliefs people have and, uh, reincarnation."

"What's that?" Ian interjected.

"Well, there's a theory we have more than one life - after we die, we come back quite often."

"Sounds like a strange idea to me," said Nancy.

"Perhaps to us here. But people in the east, China, India and so on, have believed it for years."

"Foreigners!" Ian said.

"Really? Why would anyone want to come back?" Meggie said.

"I've been asked that before." Jeremy smiled. "Sometimes we don't finish something in our lifetime or we don't get the chance to say good-bye to a loved one - that sort of thing. Others think we are on a spiritual journey and have a lot of lessons to learn - too many for one lifetime."

Ian grunted. "Sounds like some Papist nonsense."

Jeremy chuckled. "Like I said, it's a theory. I find it interesting, that's all." Jeremy put his spoon down. "The stew was excellent, Nancy. Thank you."

"There's plenty more if you want some."

"Oh no, thank you. That was quite ample."

"Well, if you're all done, why don't I show you your room. You might like to rest a while before the folks start arriving."

"That would be fine, thank you, Ian. If you could help me into my wheeled chair..."

"Of course."

The three McIntoshes watched with interest as Jeremy pushed the wheels and headed toward the door.

"I'll show you the way," said Ian, stepping ahead of him and turning right. A short distance down the hall, Ian turned into a doorway on his left. "Here you are."

Jeremy was pleasantly surprised at the size of the room. "This is quite a nice room, Ian. Thank you for arranging it for me."

"Think nothing of it. We're pleased to have a friend of Mr. Turner's staying here. If I didn't already mention it, that window looks out over the flower garden, so you can see something nice while you're sitting at the desk. Now, I'd best be gettin' to work."

"Thank you again. I'll get my things put away and join you. And, uh, if my behaviour seems a little odd, ignore it. I want to be as inconspicuous as possible. Blend into the background, if you will."

Ian nodded. "I understand," he said, his puzzled look belying his words.

Chapter 11

Hawkesbury Manor, July 1587

A scant week after Jeremy's departure, Mary feigned ill-ness to get out of her morning ride with Catherine, but as soon as her cousin galloped off, she came downstairs and headed to the stables. Mary entered quietly and stood admiring the muscles in Donald's arms as he carried heavy buckets of water to the stalls. She walked down to where he was talking softly to a horse.

"You're very fond of the horses, aren't you?" Mary said.

Donald started at the sound of her voice. "I'm sorry, Miss. I didn't hear you come in."

"I didn't mean to startle you," Mary said.

"That's all right. And yes, I am very fond of the horses. They are magnificent animals."

Mary lowered her eyelids and slowly opened them. "I can see you are very gentle with them. You have wonderful hands." Mary stepped closer and stroked the back of his left hand, which still rested on the horse's neck.

Donald's eyes travelled from her face to the top of her breasts showing above the low-cut blue dress and back to her face. "That's kind of you to say, Miss."

"Mary, please."

"Mary."

"Perhaps you would be kind enough to show me around the barn. I haven't been in here before."

"It would be a pleasure, Miss ... er, Mary. There isn't much to see, but I could show you the tack room and where the hay is stored."

"That sounds delightful."

Donald talked about the horses as they passed each stall, giving Mary a brief rundown of the horse's demeanour and characteristics. In the tack room, she pretended interest in the assortment of bridles, saddles and other equipment.

Leaving the stable proper, Donald led her into the hay barn next door which was not completely full due to the time of year, he explained.

Mary suddenly lurched forward and grabbed Donald's arm to stop falling. "Oh ... The floor's a little slippery," she said, staggering against him. Automatically, he encircled her back with his other arm.

They stood for a moment in silence, their eyes locked together.

"Are you all right?" Donald said.

"Yes. Thank you."

Donald released her and Mary took a step away, but staggered again. Once more, Donald took hold of her.

"Oh, I think I've hurt my ankle," she said. "Perhaps we could sit for a minute?"

Donald looked around. "Well, there's no place to sit here. Would you like me to carry you up to the house?"

"Oh no," she answered quickly. "I'm sure I'll be fine in a few minutes." Mary put her arms around his neck. "Perhaps you have a room somewhere close?"

"I really think it would be better if I took you back to the house."

"No, really, I ..."

Donald didn't give her a chance to finish but picked her up easily. Despite her disappointment, Mary snuggled her head under his chin, determined to make the most of the situation. He headed toward the kitchen.

"No! No. Not there. Take me to the front door, please."

"But ..."

"I insist."

Donald opened the door and stood Mary inside. "I'm sorry, my boots are dirty, so I can't come any further. Can you make it to a chair?"

"Yes. Thank you, Donald." Mary closed the door and stamped her so-called hurt foot on the floor. She went up to her room still annoyed, but after reflecting on the encounter and thinking how good she felt in Donald's arms, she smiled and tossed her head. "Not such a bad start, after all," she said aloud.

The next day, Mary again went to the stables looking for Donald. Instead, she met Bobby coming out of a stall.

"Good morning, miss. Can I help you?" he asked politely, doffing his cap.

"I need to ... um ... ask Donald something. Would you get him for me?"

"I'm sorry, miss. Donald's not here. He went to town to get some supplies."

"Oh. When will he be back?"

"I'm not sure, miss. Sometimes he's gone for a really long time like."

"I see. I'll come back this afternoon."

"Uh ... he might not be here by then, miss."

"How long can it possibly take to go into town and get supplies?"

"Uh, well, uh, he might make a couple more stops like."

Mary glared at the young lad. "Where?"

"I'm sure I don't know, miss. Er, I got to get to them horses," Bobby said, turning away and hurrying down through the barn.

Mary frowned, turned on her heel and went back to the house. Thoughts of where Donald was and what he might be doing swirled through her head. Did he have some female friend in town he was visiting? And what might that visit entail?

As Mary came into the hall, Catherine approached from the kitchen.

"Oh. Mary! There you are. I didn't bother calling for you this morning in case you were still feeling poorly," Catherine said.

"What? Oh. No, I'm fine."

"Oh good. Then I shall call you tomorrow."

"Uh, actually I don't want to go riding every morning anymore ... at least not every day. When I want to ride, I'll come along to the stables."

"That's fine. Whatever you wish. I'm sure William will be very disappointed when you don't show up."

"I couldn't care less how William feels. I don't ever want to see him again."

"Really. I know he's a bit of a bore, but he means well," Catherine said. "Would you like to have a game of chess or draughts with me?"

Mary frowned. "I don't know how to play chess and I don't want to play draughts now. I have a slight headache."

Catherine looked a little confused. It seemed Mary couldn't make up her mind whether she felt fine or not. "Sorry to hear that. When you feel better, I could show you how to play chess."

"All right. I'm going to my room to lie down."

Catherine called after her. "If you are improved later, perhaps a game of tennis? I learned how to play when I was in France."

Mary looked over the banister. "Tennis??! I think it's far too warm to play tennis." She continued on upstairs.

"Bother. That girl has more excuses than a duck has ducklings! I shall have to go and see what Richard is doing."

Chapter 12

Hawkesbury Manor, July 1587

For the next two days, Mary tried unsuccessfully to see Donald. By the third day, she was very frustrated and marched purposefully into the barn. She checked all the stalls on one side of the stable and was about to look on the other, when Donald's voice made her jump.

"Are you looking for me?" he called, stepping out of a stall.

"Oh! You startled me."

"Sorry. Didn't mean to make you jump. Bobby says you've been looking for me, to ask me something." He picked up a large pail and dumped some grain into the feeding trough.

"Yes, well ... I ... you've made me forget ..."

He raised his eyebrows and smiled at her discomfort. "Perhaps I can help you remember. Was it about your ankle? Is it better now?"

"My ankle? Oh ... uh ... yes," it's fine. Thank you."

"Good. I'm glad to hear that." He added a little more grain to the trough. "Was there something else?"

Mary reached out and touched his arm. "Uh, no. I wanted to thank you for taking care of me. I, uh, thought we could be friends. Catherine never wants to spend any time with me, and I thought you couldn't be busy all the time, so ..." Her voice trailed off.

"I'm not sure how the household would feel about you being friends with the hired help." Donald patted the horse's head.

"I don't think they would care one whit. But if you don't want to talk to me, I won't come by any more." Mary tossed her head.

"I'd be happy to talk to you whenever I have time, miss."

"Mary." She smiled and looked up at him from under her eyelids.

"Right. Mary. That's a pretty name and suits you well. You'll have to excuse me though, I have work to do now."

Mary was taken aback. "Surely it won't matter if you spend a little more time talking to me," she said, pouting slightly.

"I'm afraid it would. Taking care of the animals' needs comes first." He picked up the pail and moved toward the next stall.

"Really?! In that case, ..." Mary turned on her heel and marched out of the barn.

Animals are more important, are they, she thought. What nerve!

Mary fumed in her room for some time over this insult. He certainly wasn't acting like the other young men she had met.

Rain splattered against the windows the next morning, distorting Mary's view of the stables. A visit there would not be feasible through the mud, she thought, paying no attention to her cousin who, while waiting for Mary to take her turn at the draughts game, was animatedly talking about the great adventures her sea-faring brother John was having in some uncivilized part of the world.

"I can't understand why you wouldn't want to go to somewhere like that. Imagine being out in the wilds, seeing different exotic creatures and plants. Our cousin Francis has brought back all sorts of spices and jewels for the Queen, so I've been told." She paused. "It's your turn, Mary."

Mary looked at Catherine with a blank expression. "What?"

"Oh for heaven's sake! Pay attention. It's your turn."

"I really don't want to play this beastly game. I have a head-ache. I'm going to my room."

"I think if you didn't stay cooped up in your room all the time, you mightn't have so many headaches."

"I can't help it if I have the frail and delicate disposition of normal women, unlike some others," Mary said, turning on her heel and walking away.

Catherine rolled her eyes. What a bore!

Much to Mary's chagrin, the rain continued through the following day, finally ending by nightfall.

The next morning, Mary decided to pay a quick visit to the stables to see if Donald would agree to going on a picnic when he had some spare time. She found him standing outside a stall patting and talking to one of the horses.

"Good morning," she called.

Donald turned, looked at her appraisingly and continued stroking the horse's head.

Mary came up beside him and touched his arm. She cleared her throat.

"I was wondering ..."

Donald looked at her, his dark eyes boring into hers as he placed his hand on her arm. Mary's heart beat faster as she stared back at him.

"Yes?" he said, breaking the tense silence.

"I ... I ... uh"

"Have you forgotten want you want?"

" I ... no ... yes."

"Was it this?" He put his hand behind her head and pulled her lips to his.

Caught by surprise, Mary struggled briefly. He released her and she staggered slightly. "Not that? Perhaps this then." In one fluid motion, he slipped his left arm around her back and pulled her mouth hard against his. After forcing her lips apart, he began probing the inside of her mouth with his tongue, while his right hand was busy pushing her skirt up until he found her private place.

Mary's heart pounded so loudly in her chest, she thought it would explode. Pushing hard against Donald's shoulders, she managed to pull her head back and look at him with shocked eyes. He stepped back suddenly and she fell backwards against the boards.

"What ... what ... how dare you!" she said.

Donald laughed. "Are you trying to tell me you didn't want me to do that? I could have sworn that was not the case."

Mary put her hand to her mouth and raced out of the barn, followed by Donald's laughter.

Up in her bedroom, Mary threw herself down on the bed, trying to catch her breath. Her heart was still racing. Donald's attack was not what she had been looking for, she assured herself. But somewhere, deep inside, Mary knew she had liked it, or at least the feelings his hand and tongue had aroused. After awhile, she pulled her skirt up and put her hand where Donald's had been and began to rub as he had done briefly before she pulled away. It felt good and she rubbed harder, enjoying the sensations were coursing through her body. She imagined it was Donald's hand and her excitement grew, until her body shuddered.

Mary decided she would never go to the stables again, but as the next few days went by, the memory of the excitement she had felt when his body pressed against hers haunted most of her waking moments. She began to wonder more and more what it would be like with Donald, and if they could make love in the manner she had always envisioned.

A few days after the encounter, Mary was sitting in the summerhouse with a book on her lap, pretending to read so Catherine would not disturb her, but her mind was wrestling with conflicting thoughts about Donald. She desperately wanted his touch on her body again, but how to get around to having the experience under her terms was a dilemma.

While her mind was churning, Catherine arrived with a little bread for Mr. Getaway. After she fed the fish, Catherine looked at Mary. "Hope I didn't disturb your reading."

"Not at all." She closed the book. "In fact, I was thinking I haven't been riding in a while. Perhaps I'll join you tomorrow."

Catherine's eyebrows flew up. "Oh! That is a surprise. But fine. You know when I go, so come out when you're ready."

"I'll do that."

Thoughts of what might happen when she encountered Donald the next morning kept her from falling asleep that night, but she was up early and went downstairs for breakfast. Surprisingly, her mother was already there.

"Mary! Thank goodness you've come down. I've been very worried about you," Annabelle said.

"Whyever for, mother?"

"Because I haven't seen you for days. You know I have to stay in my rooms on these beastly hot days and you haven't visited me."

"Well, I've been busy, mother. Catherine is always wanting me to play games with her or go horseback riding. There is so much to do here. I'm sorry for neglecting you, though. I promise to do better in the future."

"All right, dear. Do sit down and have something to eat. I need to be sure you're eating properly."

"Of course I am," Mary said, helping herself to some sausage and egg. "But I can't stay long. I am supposed to go riding with Catherine, and I daresay we'll encounter William."

"I'm so happy you and Catherine are getting along, although she is such an indelicate creature." Annabelle shook her head. "Who is William?" she asked.

"He's a friend of Catherine's, a neighbour actually. He usually meets up with us for a little visit during our ride. He is quite sweet on Catherine, I think."

"Oh. That's nice. I'm sure when we get home, your father will be able to find a suitable match for you too, dear." Annabelle picked up a biscuit.

"I'm in no hurry," Mary said.

Annabelle's eyes opened wide. "Really?? I was under the impression you were anxious to find a nice young man."

"I can't imagine whatever gave you that idea, mother. I am quite happy the way things are." Mary smiled inwardly, thinking of Donald.

"I'm relieved to hear that as chances are it will be quite a while before we can go home. At least, that's the impression I had from Jeremy," she said before popping the rest of the biscuit in her mouth.

"I'm glad you're pleased, mother."

The women ate in silence for a time, until Mary's impatience became too strong. "I think I've had enough to eat, mother. Would you like me to assist you up to your room?"

"Oh, that's very kind of you, dear. Thank you. I'm not getting any younger."

Together, they climbed the stairs slowly, allowing Annabelle to catch her breath every couple of steps. Once in her room, Annabelle collapsed in a chair near the window.

"Thank you dear. I'll do a little stitching for a while. The light is quite good here."

Mary looked out the window and was relieved to find it overlooked the side garden and not the stables. She kissed her mother briefly and hurried out of the room after promising to look in more often.

Lightheartedly, she hurried down the stairs, out the door and around the side of the house where she slowed to a stroll, having decided she did not want to appear to be in a hurry if Donald happened to see her coming.

Catherine was standing by her horse talking to Bobby.

"Here you are - finally," she said. "Let's go." She stepped quickly and lightly on Bobby's hands and threw her leg over Lightning.

"Where's Donald? I shall need help mounting the horse."

"I can help you, Miss," Bobby said, cupping his hands. "I'm really quite strong you know." He smiled broadly.

"Of course, you can, Bobby. Go ahead, Mary." Lightning pranced around, as impatient as Catherine to get moving.

Mary looked displeased, but acquiesced, as she didn't see any way out of it.

The horses trotted out of the yard, Lightning leading the way. Once in the field, Catherine urged her horse to a gallop. Star refused to be held back by Mary's hold on the reins. As the area became more wooded, Catherine slowed her horse to a walk, much to Mary's relief.

As expected, William was waiting at the usual spot and his face lit up when he saw Mary coming with Catherine. With a big smile, he hurried over to assist her in dismounting.

"How wonderful to see you again, Miss Mary."

"No doubt," she said.

William seemed oblivious to all Mary's rebuffs and continued to dance attendance on her all the while they were by the river. Mary could stand him no longer and rose to her feet.

"I think it's time for us to go," she said.

William looked disappointed, but hastened to offer his assistance when she approached her horse.

Mary looked pointedly at Catherine. "Do stay and ride with us, Catherine. We quite enjoy your company."

Catherine chuckled. "Of course. Be sure you keep up with me."

When they reached the stables, Bobby came hurrying out to help. Mary turned to Catherine. "Do we always have to meet that odious boy when out riding?" So engrossed was Mary in expressing her disgust, she accepted Bobby's help without thinking.

"William can go where he pleases and he's there hoping to see you. I think he's in love with you." Catherine turned to Bobby. "Thanks, Bobby. Give them a good rubdown."

"Yes, miss." He led the horses away and the girls continued up to the house.

"Nonsense! I've certainly not given him any encouragement. Besides, we've only met a few times and that's a few times too many."

"Ah well, he carries your memory close to his heart," Catherine said. "Do you care for a game of tennis in a while?" She pushed open the door.

"No, I don't think so. I need to have a rest."

"Of course you do," Catherine said.

Mary looked at her sharply, not sure if Catherine was being solicitous or sarcastic. She said nothing, however, as her main concern was making sure she could return to the stables unseen.

"Perhaps I'll see if Mrs. Stewart needs some help in the kitchen."

Mary watched as Catherine headed off to the kitchen, and then went upstairs to change her clothes.

Listening intently and hearing only silence, Mary once more made her way out of the house. When she entered the stables, she found them completely empty.

"Hello? Anyone here?"

"Just me, Miss," a voice called from the loft. "Donald's putting the horses out in the pasture."

"Thank you, Bobby. Where would that be?"

"Go out the back door, miss. Turn to your right and then past the small shed turn left. You should be able to see them."

Mary followed directions and saw Donald leaning on a fence watching the horses run around the field. Mary didn't say anything until she was right behind him. "Donald."

Donald turned, his face muscles tense as he waited for her to speak. He wondered if Richard had sent her to fire him. She gave a tentative smile.

"I'm glad you came," he said. "I really want to apologize for acting like such a boor the other day. You are a fine lady and don't deserve to be treated like a ... uh ... I'm sorry. I had overindulged in ale the night before and it made me act in a manner unlike my usual self."

"Apology accepted. You rather frightened me, you know."

"I'm sorry. I truly am."

"And perhaps I overreacted a little. I should have realized something made you behave that way."

He turned to look at the horses to hide his smile. "They are amazing animals, aren't they? So beautiful." He rested his arms on the fence. "You know what I think of when I watch them running around?"

Mary shook her head.

"Freedom. They run like wild creatures with their manes blowing out. Wouldn't it be wonderful to be able to run like that with not a care in the world?" Donald sighed.

"I didn't realize you were so … philosophical," she said, unsure if that was the right word.

"Would you care to walk a ways with me? There is a grove that will be lovely and cool," he said, indicating a stretch of oak trees. "I promise to be a gentleman."

Donald seemed like a new person and Mary did not hesitate to go with them. He was right. A few feet into the forest and the temperature dropped several degrees.

"There is a small clearing near the brook where we can sit if you like. Through here." He pushed aside the lower branches of a wych elm tree.

The clearing was indeed quite small but the grass grew abundantly from the moisture provided by the little stream.

"I'm so sorry. I don't have anything for you to sit on," Donald said.

"That's all right. The ground will do quite nicely."

Donald sat well away from her. "I don't have much spare time, but I like to come here occasionally and do a little fishing. Have you ever fished, Mary?"

"No. And I don't fancy touching slimy fish."

Donald smiled. "If you ever want to try, I will remove the fish for you. What's it like where you live? Do you miss your home?"

Mary, pleased Donald was taking an interest in her, chatted pleasantly about their estate, her father's hunting dogs and her uncle who was in the English navy. Donald listened attentively but when she finally asked him about his home, he said it was time to get back, as he had work to do.

"But you do have a home somewhere, don't you, Donald?" she persisted.

"My mother lives in town, but I stay here all the time. I have a room off the stable so I can be near the horses, and Mrs. Stewart sends my food over from the kitchen."

"Would that be through the door beside the first stall?"

"Yes." Donald fidgeted and looked back the way they had come.

"I hate to leave when it's so lovely and cool here, but I'd best be letting you get on with your work," Mary said.

Donald gave a slight bow. "Right. We can come again some time."

As she walked back to the house, Mary was surprised and confused at how disappointed she felt because Donald had not so much as touched her hand. Part of her longed for him to hold her; part of her congratulated herself as being in control.

From her bedroom window, Mary watched the stars and moon appear in the summer sky and listened to the crickets singing to each other. When all was still in the house, she crept downstairs and crossed the courtyard to the stables, keeping in the shadows of the buildings. Very little light found its way through the door and into the inside of the stable. A couple of the horses whinnied as they detected the presence of an intruder.

Mary could barely see the outline of the door on her left. She gently lifted the latch and stepped cautiously into the room. Suddenly, she was grabbed and thrown to the floor.

"Ooooow!"

"What ...?"

The moonlight filtering through the window illuminated Mary's crumpled form on the floor.

"Mary!! Oh, I'm so sorry." Donald hurried to where Mary sat in a heap and helped her up. "Are you all right? Oh God, I'm sorry. I thought you were a thief. Are you hurt?" He held her at arm's length to check.

"I'm fine. I guess it's my fault for not knocking, but I thought you might be asleep."

"No. I was lying in bed, thinking about ... you, when I heard the horses whinny. They don't usually do that unless something has come into the barn."

"You were thinking of me?" Mary said.

"Yes. I ... Is something wrong?"

"No, nothing. I was thinking about you and came out ..." her voice faltered.

Donald pulled her closer. "It seems we were thinking about each other. What were you thinking about me, Mary?" His breath was warm on her face.

"Just ... I don't ..." She leaned in against his chest. "This."

He held her tightly. "But you shouldn't be here. The family wouldn't like it."

"They don't have to know. It can be our secret."

Donald put his hand under her head and pulled her mouth to his. The kiss was long and demanding, and what little hesitancy he felt at first dissipated into a fiery longing.

To Mary, it seemed as if her entire being melted into Donald's. She was breathless when he pulled back momentarily, looking deeply into her eyes. Satisfied at what he saw, he reached into the top of her dress, freeing one breast from its hiding place. He took the nipple in his mouth, sucking and licking. Mary groaned as waves of pleasure raced through her body. He released the other breast and squeezed and rubbed it, then circled the nipple with his tongue. Returning to her mouth, Donald kissed her deeply again. Mary could feel his male hardness pushing against her.

Donald leaned away and looked down at her. He could see the beat of her racing heart. Gently, he raised her to her feet, and with a speed faster than Mary could have imagined possible, he removed her gown and petticoat, leaving her standing naked before his gaze. Just as swiftly, his shirt and trousers were thrown aside and he watched Mary's eyes grow large as she took in the size of his manhood.

He picked her up and laid her down on his bed. She pulled his face to hers, delighting in the wonder of his lips.

"Easy, my love," he said, stroking her face. Softly, he kissed her lips, sensuously moving his mouth around hers, while his hand trailed over her shoulder, down her arm and returning to her breast. He began a slow journey down her torso, kissing and licking while caressing her inner thigh. Mary shuddered. He travelled up her body, and as his tongue darted around her mouth, Donald locked his fingers in hers and gently extended her arms up on either side of her head.

He moved his head down to kiss her throat, at the same time releasing his hand and letting it trail down her arm, once again coming to rest on her breast. He cupped it in his hand and began sucking the nipple, now erect under his touch. Mary's breath was quick and erratic and she gasped in ecstasy.

Donald kissed her mouth, while his hand slipped past the silken hair to the warm, moist spot between her legs. He began a blazing trail of kisses from her throat to her abdomen, a passionate journey to the secret garden. Having opened the door with his fingers, Donald's tongue began its exploration. Mary moaned softly, writhing as the touch of his tongue shot ripples of electricity through her body. Her back arched and her mound thrust upwards against his mouth. Desire flooded every inch of her being.

Donald raised himself up and slowly slipped his throbbing member into her, thrusting faster and faster until they cried out together at the height of their passion. His energy drained, Donald rested lightly against her and kissed her tenderly. As he made to move off, Mary's arms tightened around him.

"Not yet."

"Not yet? How long should I stay like this?"

"Forever."

Donald smiled. "That might be a little awkward."

She gazed up at him in wonder and ran one hand down the side of his face.

"I didn't know this would be so wonderful," Mary said.

He kissed her again passionately and, as he rolled away, drew her within the circle of his arms. They snuggled together, Mary savoring the closeness, wanting the moment to last forever. The sleep which is the aftermath of passion, overcame them. Their bodies remained close and a smile of happiness played across Mary's face, even as she slept, dreaming of the many summer nights to follow.

Chapter 13

Hawkesbury Manor, Late July 1587

Wishing to allay any concerns her cousin might have over her activities, Mary elected one morning to join Catherine on her daily ride. As Donald helped her up onto the horse, Mary whispered, "I'll see you soon."

Catherine looked impatiently back at her cousin. "Oh do come along."

Mary glowered at her, but Catherine missed the look as she had turned her horse and was trotting off. Shortly before reaching their usual spot by the river, Mary called out to Catherine.

"Wait! Stop!"

Catherine reined in and turned back to Mary. "What's wrong?"

"I'm going back to the house. I'm not feeling well."

"That's too bad. I know William would love to see you. Every day I arrive and you're not with me, he looks so woebegone. Won't you come along and at least say hello to the poor boy?"

"You know perfectly well, I have no desire to speak to William now or at any time in the future."

"He'll probably die of a broken heart," Catherine said. "And it will be your fault." She laughed.

"Don't care if he does," Mary retorted. "I'll see you later."

Catherine watched her cousin ride off. "Lightning," she said, "if I live to be one hundred I'll never understand that girl or what she does with her time. Let's go," she said, patting his neck.

Donald came out when Mary arrived back at the stable. "You're back early."

"Because I have special plans for us today."

"And what might those be?" he said, helping her down.

"You'll see. I'll be back in a minute."

Mary hurried off to the house and came back minutes later carrying a basket. She went into the barn where Donald was finishing up with Star.

"What's this all about then?"

"I thought we might go to your special spot by the creek and have some lunch," Mary said, indicating the basket.

"You should warn me about these things. I can't always walk away when I feel like it." Donald sounded annoyed.

Mary pouted and looked up from under her lashes. "Don't scold me. I wanted it to be a surprise."

"I guess it's all right this time," he said grudgingly.

Donald's mood improved as they neared the creek. "It is rather nice to have a break during the day."

"Of course it is."

Mary spread a blanket and removed the contents of the basket - bread, cheese, eggs, chicken and a flagon of wine.

"How did you manage to get all that together without Mrs. Stewart's seeing you?"

"I went to the kitchen before she was up."

They ate their food in silence until everything was gone.

"That was nice, Mary. I have a surprise for you too."

"What's that?"

"Something you haven't seen yet - at least I don't think you have. Come on."

He took her hand and set off up the creek from where they had been sitting. The creek widened into a rolling river, its surface bubbly white where it drove against a checkerboard of stones. Rumbling, low at first, grew louder the closer they got to a curve in the river.

"What is that noise?"

"Part of my surprise, Mary. Hurry up and see."

As they rounded the bend, the source of the sound was revealed. A cascade of rapidly falling water, dazzlingly brilliant in the bright sun, threw a fine mist into the air before churning the water at the bottom into a bubbling white foam. Mary's eyes widened and a smile lit up her face. "A waterfall! How lovely!"

"Not just a waterfall. Follow me."

Donald began to climb the hill beside the waterfall, then stopped. The mist, heavier now, settled over them.

Mary wiped her hand across her face. "Where are you going? We'll fall in."

"Trust me."

Mary held tightly to his hand and followed him under the waterfall and into a passageway which veered to the left and ended in a cave illuminated by sunlight shining through an opening in the ceiling. In the middle of the room was a large pool, its surface a floor where sunbeams danced to the music of tiny ripples. A continuous stream of water lazily fed the pool through an opening in the wall a few feet above the ground while a small channel vanished into the rock near where they were standing.

"How beautiful! Who would have thought such a thing existed."

"I found it many years ago by accident," Donald said. "What say we go for a swim in the pool?"

"I can't swim."

"You don't have to. The deepest spot is only about four feet. We can leave our clothes here. I'll race you." Donald was out of his clothes long before Mary and she found herself approaching the pool under Donald's admiring gaze.

"I'll help you in." He took her by the waist and swung her into the water, inhaling the musky scent of her body as he pressed her abdomen to his face before setting her down.

"It's not very warm," she said.

"A little cool, but it gets warmer as the day goes on. Move around a bit." Donald did a few strokes to the channel and back. He put his arms around Mary, drew her to him and kissed her. "Does that warm you up a little?"

"A little."

"Let me sit you on the edge." Donald lifted her back onto the edge of the pool. "Is that better?"

"Much. I don't mind my feet being in the water."

"Speaking of your feet ..."

Donald lifted her left foot, massaged it gently and kissed it. He did the same with the other, grasped both her ankles and slowly ran his hands up the outside of her legs, massaging them and spreading them apart as he went. Beyond her knees, his hands switched their route to the inside of her legs, where he caressed and kissed them. Mary's back arched and she leaned backward on her hands. With great deliberation, he moved his hands up to her hips, using a circular motion with his thumbs to massage the sensitive groin area.

Mary's breathing quickened as Donald brought his hands up to her breasts, cupping and kissing them. Mary bent forward to reach his mouth. Their tongues played together, circling lips and mouth. He kissed her cheeks and eyes, returned to her mouth and began a trip down her neck, fully exposed as she lifted her chin.

Again he kissed her breasts, followed by a zigzag trail of kisses down her body, culminating at the entrance to her secret garden, where he drew his tongue repeatedly up the length of the lips before parting them and flicking it rapidly against her highly erogenous zone. Mary groaned and threw herself backwards on the rock slab, her breath shallow and frequent. Donald probed deeper inside her and Mary cried aloud. Donald leaned back and Mary sat upright. He put his hands around her waist and lifted her down onto his waiting member, pushing her back against the side of the pool as he thrust into her. Their cries of release came at the same time.

With slackened bodies, Donald kissed Mary long and tenderly. She collapsed against his shoulder before pulling back and smiling at him.

Without speaking, he lifted her out of the water, so she was once again sitting on the side of the pool. He hoisted himself up beside her.

"I'm guessing you're not cold now," he said, smiling.

"No." She smiled back.

"Time to go," Donald said. "Let's get dressed."

Mary pouted. "Already? I don't want to go back yet." She put her hand on Donald's shoulder.

Impatiently, he pushed it away. "We have to. It's a work day for me, remember?"

She rubbed her hand, frowning. "All right," she said, getting to her feet.

Mary turned her back to Donald as she dressed. She had just finished, when he pushed her hair aside and kissed the back of her neck. Her annoyance vanished as she turned to him, smiling. "This was a lovely surprise. Thank you."

"And you for providing the lunch."

As they were leaving the cave, Mary looked back. "This is our own special private place," she said. "Right?"

"Right." Donald kept to himself the thoughts of the many other women who believed this was their own "private" place.

Chapter 14

Hawkesbury Manor, Late August 1587

"I miss Jemmy." Catherine leaned on an unfinished table watching Richard work on a chair. "It seems like he's been gone forever rather than a few weeks." She sighed.

"I miss him too," Richard said. "You look so sad. Would you like me to ... would you mind if ..."

"What? Why are you mumbling?"

"I wondered if you would like me to hold you - you know, give you a hug?"

Catherine looked surprised. "A hug?" Her brow furrowed, then cleared. "Well, why not?"

He came over and pulled her against his chest. Catherine could feel his heart beating. With his arms encircling her, Catherine suddenly realized how comfortable she felt and a warm feeling ran through her body. Such feelings were so surprising and foreign, they made her jump back.

Richard's arms dropped. "What's wrong?"

"Nothing, I think I'm, uh, coming down with a fever," Catherine said, unwilling to admit the truth.

"You do look a little flushed. Why don't you sit down?" Richard took her arm and held it till she sat. "I have some water here." He hurried to a side table, poured a glass of water from the carafe and brought it to her.

"Thank you." She took a sip. He continued to hover. "I'm fine now, thank you, Richard."

"Are you sure?"

"Yes, of course. I wouldn't say so if it weren't true," Catherine said, and realized she had just finished telling an untruth. She coughed and quickly changed the subject. "So who are you making the chair for?"

"Captain and Mrs. Prentice. They have ordered two, actually."

"It looks quite lovely already." Catherine looked around the room.

"You do amazing things with wood, Richard."

"Thank you, Catherine. It is a gift with which I have been blessed."

They sat in comfortable silence for several minutes. Richard stopped working and wiped his brow. "Where's Mary this afternoon?"

"I don't know and really don't care as long as she isn't bothering me. Actually, I haven't seen much of her for the past several weeks. I don't know what she does - sleeps probably. She still comes riding with me some mornings ... if she can haul herself out of bed. I never saw a person sleep so much. It seems to be her favourite thing."

"Maybe she has some kind of illness."

"Could be. I have no idea." Catherine crossed her legs. "I'm quite happy she doesn't come riding too often because she is so mean to William. I don't overly like him myself or anything - his face is not unlike that of his porcine father - but I would never act toward him as she does."

"What does she do?"

"Snubs him. He is always very polite and gentlemanly, treats her with respect and she acts like he is a bug that needs squishing. I know his feelings get hurt because he really likes Mary. One could almost say he's in love with her." She opened her eyes wide. "Well, he would be if she gave him half a chance. Really, I don't blame her for not loving William. Like I said, he reminds me of his father. I can imagine his children will look like a litter of piglets."

Richard burst out laughing. "Oh, Cathy! I'm sure any offspring he has will be perfectly normal." He continued laughing as he polished the seat of the chair.

Catherine smiled. "Anyway, we can be sure Mary will not be the mother of them, whatever they look like. She has made it perfectly clear she wants nothing to do with William. Not that her actions have deterred him. He still looks at her like a lovesick cow. Maybe someday if he hears she is married to someone else, he will join a monastery, or perhaps languish away in his room, never to see the light of day again."

Richard laughed. "Does she have a gentleman friend back home?"

"No. I don't know why, except she mentioned her father keeps her under lock and key, so to speak, and she is perfectly man-crazy, if that's a word. Men seem to be all she ever thinks about. Perfectly boring. There are so many more interesting things to think about."

"Do you not think about your future, Cathy - about marrying and having children?" Richard looked up from his work.

"Not really. I suppose I will marry eventually some time far in the future, but I want to go places and see strange things before that happens."

Richard resumed polishing the chair seat. "What would you like to do, or where would you like to go?"

"I'd like to go where Christopher Columbus has been, or the islands where Francis Drake visits and brings such wondrous things back to England. I hear it is beautiful there and always warm."

"True, but until the fighting stops, those islands might be a dangerous place to go."

"Oh. But what about the Americas or Virginia? Jemmy says Walter Raleigh sent John White and about 100 settlers there. Or maybe Kanata?"

"I heard it can be very cold in Kanata, Catherine. I don't think you'd like that very much. He put down his rag and folded his arms across his chest. "Mind you, I must agree with you about wanting to see the new lands. I would love to. Might be dangerous in places though, because Spain controls many areas."

"I don't care. I want to go, even if I have to learn to speak Spanish and pretend to be from Spain. And if you really want to go, we can go together." She jumped up and whirled around.

Richard stared at Catherine in shock. "You cannot travel by yourself with a man to whom you are not married! Think of the scandal."

"Well, then, we will pretend to be married."

Richard chuckled. "I can just imagine Jeremy's face when you tell him that."

Catherine sighed and sat down again. "I guess there's no help for it. You will have to marry me."

Richard's face became very serious. "Cathy, I want to marry a woman who is in love with me, not someone who needs a travel escort."

"You know I love you. You are like a brother to me."

Richard felt like a rock had crushed his heart. He picked up the rag again. "It isn't brotherly love of which I speak, Catherine," he said solemnly.

"Oh. You mean ... that other thing." Catherine's face flushed. "I ... I, uh, think I need to, uh ... do something." She jumped to her feet and rushed out of the workshop.

Richard looked wistfully at the chair. "If only she did love me." He sighed. "Maybe some day."

Chapter 15

The Crown & Anchor, Early September 1587

The summer had passed quickly for Jeremy, with most of his days spent in the garden with Meggie. When he discovered she could neither read nor write, he offered to teach her the alphabet. Meggie was a quick learner and was overjoyed the day she learned to spell her own name. He read to her from some of his books on reincarnation and they had lengthy discussions on that subject as well as on the state of affairs in England regarding the ongoing war with Spain.

Meggie and her family delighted in his fiddle playing and during the times when the tavern was closed, Jeremy would play for their enjoyment. It was a pleasant time and eased the pain of missing his family. Although Ian had pressed him to play in the tavern, Jeremy had firmly refused, using shyness as an excuse. In truth, he did not wish to draw attention to himself nor, on the off-chance that someone who had seen him at the Boar's Head would happen to come in, did he wish to help stir up an old memory.

By autumn, Jeremy realized he was in love with Meggie, but kept his feelings to himself. He found her sitting in the garden one morning staring into space.

"Good morning, Meggie. You're looking a little sad. Is something wrong?"

"Oh! I ... it's just that I can smell the Fall today and this time of year always makes me feel a little sad."

"Why is that?"

"I don't know, really. It just does. Besides, I was thinking about you and that you will be leaving us ... sometime." Meggie stared off into space.

"I don't think my leaving here will be any time soon. Will it upset you when I have to go, Meggie?" Jeremy tried to see her face.

"Of course it will. I ... we will miss you terribly. It has been wonderful having you here."

"I would certainly miss you too. All of you. But especially you, Meggie."

Meggie turned and looked at him, her face flushed. "Really?"

"Of course. I've grown very fond of you."

Meggie looked down at her hands. "And I of you, Thomas."

"Meggie, look at me. I am crippled. I have never anticipated having a normal life with ... anyone, let alone a beautiful woman like you."

"I have eyes. I know what I see. And that is an attractive, intelligent young man," Meggie said sharply. "At least I think there's one under that awful scruffy beard," she continued in a friendlier tone.

Meggie pulled his beard. Jeremy chuckled. "It is rather a mess, isn't it?"

"As to having a normal life, what has been more normal than your life for the past two months?"

"Yes, I understand what you mean, but I was referring to ...uh... let's say for instance, expecting a woman to be wanting to spend her life with me. You know ... when I can't walk."

"Whyever wouldn't I ... she, I mean?"

"Well, I just thought ..."

Meggie put her hands on her hips. "Seems to me you didn't think at all, Thomas! Any woman would be lucky to have you for a husband - unless there's more about you I should know. Perhaps you have a wife locked away in a tower somewhere."

Jeremy laughed. "You remind me of Cath ... I mean someone else who has a vivid imagination."

Meggie looked at him thoughtfully. "If you think I need enlightening, why don't you tell me something about yourself, Thomas?"

"It's true you really don't know anything about me, Meggie, and for very good reasons which I can't reveal now, I can't tell you anything. Someday, but just not now. I'm sorry. Please understand."

"All right. But I will hold you to your promise to reveal your horrible, dark secrets." Meggie smiled. "Meanwhile, I would like some tea. How about you?"

"Sounds like a wonderful idea."

Meggie stood and put her face close to his. "Just remember - I think you're a perfectly fine young man, Thomas." She suddenly kissed him on the forehead and hurried away to the kitchen.

Jeremy's heart leaped. The day suddenly grew brighter and warmer. For the first time, he wished he weren't involved in this spying role or, at least that something would happen to make it end soon.

Meggie returned with the tea. After she had placed the tray on the table, Jeremy took her hand.

"Meggie, you are so lovely. I never expected to meet anyone like you, and if you really meant what you said about any woman wanting to have a life with me ... I know this is soon, but ..."

"Ye forgot the plate of cookies, Meggie," Nancy McIntosh said as she came around the corner.

Meggie whirled around, pulling her hand out of Jeremy's.

"Oh, so I did. Thank you, Mum."

"They smell wonderful, Nancy, just like all your cooking. A man eating your delicious meals could end up looking like our late King Henry VIII."

"Flattery won't get you any more of yon cookies, young Thomas," Nancy said, smiling. She sniffed exuberantly. "There's cool in the air and I can smell Fall coming for sure. Next thing you know, it will be harvest time and all they drunkards will be a-banging on the door at three in the morning, disturbing hard-workin' folk from their bed."

"Good thing Fall comes only once a year then, Nancy."

"Aye, ye're right about that. I'd best be gettin' along. Drink up yer tea, Meggie, and come give me a hand with tonight's stew, luv."

Nancy stood, waiting. Meggie looked at Jemmy and raised her eyebrows. She swallowed the last of her tea.

"Coming, Mummy. Shall I pour you another cup, Thomas, before I take the tray away?"

"Yes, please."

"And leave the cookies for him, Meggie. He's a growing boy." Nancy laughed at her own joke.

"I'll be sure to bring the plate in when I come," Jemmy said.

"He's well-trained, our Thomas, eh, Meggie."

Meggie smiled at Jeremy before disappearing around the corner.

The evening passed as uneventfully as all the previous. Jeremy remained huddled at his table, his thoughts full of his conversation with Meggie that afternoon. After closing, Ian brought him his wheeled chair and pushed him to his room.

"It's pretty chilly out this evenin', laddie. I'll just light the fire for ye."

"Thank you, Ian. The dampness does bother my legs a bit."

"There you are, Thomas, all set for the night, unless there's something else I can do for you."

"No thanks, Ian. Have a pleasant sleep and, God willing, we'll see each other in the morning."

"Indeed. Have a good sleep yerself, laddie."

Sleep did not come quickly to Jeremy, as a multitude of thoughts tumbled through his mind. It seemed like hours had gone by when he heard the door quietly open. Yellow fingers of flickering candlelight pushed against the darkness where the dying fire could not reach.

"Thomas?" a voice called softly. "Thomas, it's me, Meggie. Are you awake?"

"Yes. Come in, Meggie." Jeremy turned to lean on his elbow.

Stepping through the door as quietly as her rustling skirts would allow, Meggie approached the bed. "I was afraid I might wake you." She set the candle on the table.

"No, I haven't been asleep yet."

"Nor have I."

"It's late, Meggie. Are you ill? Is something wrong with your parents?"

"No, no. Everyone's fine. I just couldn't sleep, thinking about what you said, or almost said, today. Then I began to wonder if, that is, I might have misunderstood what you meant."

Jeremy hesitated. "Meggie, I haven't told you this. I have no right to tell you now. But I care for you - no, more than that. I love you, Meggie. You are the sweetest girl I've ever met." Jeremy fell back and turned his head away. "Oh, God forgive me for saying that."

Meggie's heart thumped in her chest. She sat on the edge of the bed, gently turned his head and cupped his face in her hands. "Look at me, Thomas. Are you telling me true? You really love me?"

"Yes, although it's not fair for me to say so. I cannot promise you a future, Meggie, when it's so uncertain for me at the moment. In another lifetime, the outlook might be better. Maybe I'll be a simple countryman with two good legs who does nothing but tend sheep. Right now, I just don't know what will happen. Besides, I couldn't ask you to spend the rest of your life with a cripple."

"Don't you ever talk like that again, Thomas Smithson! Next lifetime indeed! Sheep herder, yet! Well, it's this lifetime I'm thinking about, and God may not have seen fit to make your legs work properly, but you're a fine man, good-natured and pleasant to be around. Any woman would be lucky and proud to have a future with you, and if you're asking, then I'm saying 'yes.'"

She leaned to kiss him and his arms encircled her lovingly. As their kiss deepened, the embers that had smoldered for so long ignited into the flames of passion.

Moaning softly, Jeremy pulled back. "You don't even know who I really am, Meggie, and I cannot tell you yet."

"I know what I've seen of you since you've been here, and that's good enough for me, Thomas. Whatever else you have to tell can be said at a later time."

"Oh, Meggie. I do love you so, but what will your parents say?"

"They will say I am a very lucky young woman to have found such a fine man." Meggie stood and started unlacing the ties of her dress.

"What ... " Jeremy began and then was silent, as the dress fell off her shoulders revealing her full breasts, nipples erect with anticipation. In one movement, Meggie removed her undergarment and stood naked before him, her body a luminescent pink in the glow of the fire. Candlelight was reflected in her eyes as she waited while Jeremy's glance roamed over her voluptuous curves, ending in the shadows of her legs. When he looked back at her face, desire smouldered in his eyes.

Speaking not a word, Meggie blew out the candle and swiftly climbed into the bed. Jeremy pulled her soft body against his. "Meggie, you are so beautiful."

Once more their lips met and this time there was no quenching the fire that consumed their bodies. Their love-making continued until both fell into a deep, happy sleep, wrapped in each other's arms.

Chapter 16

M ary paced up and down her room, the deep crease in her forehead defining her anxiety. Her mind was a whirlwind of thoughts. Could this really be happening? Didn't Donald do anything to protect me? The more she thought, the angrier she became until at last she raced out of the house and down to the stables.

"Donald! Donald! Where are you?"

"Gads, I'm right here. Stop all that yelling. You're scaring the horses."

Donald came toward her. "What's the matter?"

Mary grabbed his arms. "I'll tell you what's the matter. I'm with child, that's what."

"What's that got to do with me?" He shrugged his shoulders and started to walk away.

Mary grabbed his arm and turned him around. "It has every-thing to do with you. It's your fault!"

Donald's eyes opened wide as he shoved her hand away. "MY fault? Who threw herself at me at every opportunity? Who came sneaking into my room in the middle of the night like a common prostitute? I never asked you to lift your skirts. It was your idea."

Mary's mouth dropped open. "I ... but ... I thought you had done something to stop this from happening."

"What did you think I had done or expect me to do?"

"I don't know. Whatever is necessary. You could have said it wasn't a good idea." Mary's eyes welled.

Donald laughed. "You are making a joke, I think. You wanted me, I obliged. But I might have a solution for you."

"What?" Mary said, sniffling.

"You could do what my other women do - get rid of it."

This was the last thing Mary expected to hear. "What?! Your 'other' women! There are others? Get rid of it? What?"

"Surely you didn't think you were the only woman I bed?" Donald laughed. "Silly girl. And yes, get rid of it. There is something you can take, unless you have a better plan."

Mary was shocked and stood silently trying to understand what Donald had just told her. He watched the emotions fleeting across her face.

"I can get you a potion that will get rid of it just like it never happened. There could be complications, of course, but most of them are only sick for a little while."

"I ... I don't know ..."

"Think about it and when you do 'know', tell me. Meanwhile, I'm busy now." Donald walked away.

Mary stood there, momentarily paralyzed and speechless. Like an automaton, she turned and went back to her room. Her confusion turned to fury as she thought over all he had said. How dare he bed other women while making passionate love to me?! And take something to get rid of it? Out of the question. Mother would be full of questions if I were sick. There had to be another solution.

A tapping on the door was followed by Catherine's voice. "Mary? Are you all right? May I come in?"

Mary did not answer immediately as she tried to calm down. Catherine knocked again. "Mary?"

"Very well," she said, turning her back to the door.

"I saw you come in and you looked quite upset. Is there anything wrong?" Catherine headed across the room.

"No, everything's fine," Mary turned again so Catherine could not see her face.

Catherine stopped, uncertain of what to do. She decided to push on. "Oh. Well, I'm glad to hear that. I don't know whether it will interest you or not, but I have some news. A young lad from the Harrisons came by with an invitation to attend a party, a harvest festival sort of thing. They do it every year. It's quite jolly, with a big bonfire and everything. It will be a week from tomorrow starting in the afternoon. I wondered if you would like to attend."

"The Harrisons?"

"Yes. You know - William's parents. Richard and I will be going. Your mother is welcome too, of course. I think it might do you good to get out of the house for a while and have some fun. What do you think?"

Mary's first inclination was to say no, but an idea suddenly popped into her head. William. She finally looked at Catherine and smiled. "I think that would be quite pleasant. I will go with you."

Catherine's eyes opened wide. "A good decision, Mary. It will be a lovely change for you. We'll be leaving around noonday. After I talk to your mother, I'll send Bobby with a message to say we're coming."

"Very well. I'll look forward to it."

"Excellent. I'll go speak to Aunt Annabelle." Catherine went out the door, deciding she would never understand Mary's whims.

Mary lay down on her bed mulling over the idea that had come to her when Catherine mentioned William. She had no doubt she could seduce him and force him to marry her. The thought of William touching her made her shiver with disgust, but the end result would be preferable to anything else she could think of.

The Monday before the celebration, Mary told Catherine she would accompany her on her morning ride. As expected, when they rode into the clearing, William was waiting. His face lit up with pleasure when he saw Mary; he smiled and hurried over to help her down. Much to his surprise, she favoured him with a big smile and held his arms a little longer than necessary.

"Thank you, William," she said demurely. "That is so kind of you."

"You are welcome, I'm sure. Please come sit on the blanket I have."

William's plain face flushed with pleasure.

"Only if you agree to sit beside me," Mary said, fluttering her lashes.

Catherine's mouth fell open.

"You must tell me how you've been. I haven't seen you for so long. What have you been doing?" Mary asked.

"Well, I ... um ... I ... oh just the usual things, you know ... helping to tend the garden ... uh."

Mary appeared to be hanging on every word, although she was unsure of what to reply, gardening being an area with which she was totally unfamiliar.

Catherine found her tongue. "William is an expert on herbs. He grows quite a collection of them each year and is kind enough to give some to Mrs. Stewart for use in our kitchen, which accounts in part for the wonderful flavours you can taste in the food she prepares."

"Really! How delightful! You must show me your garden when we come next week." The insincere words dripped like honey from her mouth.

"I'd be delighted, if you wouldn't be bored."

"Bored?" Mary leaned toward William, touched his arm and smiled. "Silly boy. How could I possibly be bored in your delightful company," she said flirtatiously.

Catherine made a choking sound, then cleared her throat. "Sorry."

"Speaking of next week, I gather there will be dancing in the evening?"

Mary smiled coquettishly.

William's senses were aflame to the extent that his chest tightened and he could hardly breathe. "Why, yes. First, we will watch the villagers dancing out near the fire and then go inside for a ball and midnight feast."

"I hope you will save a dance or two for me," Mary said, smiling and batting her eyes even more at William.

William's breath was coming in short gasps. "Every dance shall be with you, if you wish, my dear Mary," he said smiling broadly.

"I think it's time we went home. Lunch will be ready soon," Catherine said.

"Oh, must we go so soon? I was having such a delightful time talking to William," Mary said, pouting and looking at William with feigned longing.

William flushed. "Perhaps you will come again tomorrow," he said hopefully, as he reached for her hand.

"If you want me to, I shall certainly come, if I feel well," Mary said, trying not to shudder at his touch.

"Oh. If you are ill, you must not tire yourself out," William said hastily.

When the girls parted ways with William, Mary turned back to look at him and blew him a kiss. William was so dazzled he froze in his saddle. After she turned away, he cursed himself for his clumsiness in not returning her kiss.

As he had earlier, Bobby came to help Mary dismount and take the horses inside.

On their way to the house, Catherine turned to Mary. "What in the world was that all about with William?"

"I have no idea what you're talking about." Mary put her head in the air and kept on walking.

Catherine stopped momentarily, her mouth agape, and stared at Mary's retreating back. She hurried to catch up, and grabbed Mary's arm. "The way you were acting with William. I'm a little confused. I thought you didn't like him."

Mary tossed her head and pulled her arm out of Catherine's grasp. "I don't know where you got that idea." She brushed at her sleeve. "There's nothing wrong with William. He's just a little ... shy."

"But ..."

"I don't want to hear another word about it. He likes me and I like him. That's all there is to it. If you are jealous, I can't help it."

"Jealous?? Of William?" Catherine's laugh turned into a snort. "That is the most ridiculous thing I've ever heard! I have no interest in William other than as a friend."

"Good then. We shall say no more."

Catherine shook her head as she followed her cousin into the house. I don't think I will ever understand Mary. Next Saturday should be very interesting.

Chapter 17

Hawkesbury Manor, Late September 1587

Mary stared out the window as the coach drove sedately down the long drive to Harrison Hall. Her eyes grew large as she took in the enormous edifice three stories high, with six turrets reaching to the sky, two on the corners, the other four evenly spaced across the front. Triple chimney pots popped up above the roof in several locations.

As a footman helped the girls down from the carriage, Mary continued to stare at the place she had already determined would be hers some day. "I had no idea William lived in a castle like this," she said, all agog.

"Really? What else would an Earl and Countess live in?"

"Earl and Countess??! Really? I didn't know." Mary's heart raced as she realized marriage to William would not only solve her problem, but put her in the nobility class.

William had been anxiously waiting on the front steps and hurried to greet them, followed closely by a medium-sized brown and beige dog, his tail carried high and waving in delight. "Hello ladies. So happy you could come. Mary, you look absolutely enchanting," he said, kissing her hand.

Mary backed away from the dog, who looked puzzled, then remembered her mission and smothered her repulsion to both William and the four-legged creature. "Thank you, William. What is that?" she said, pointing to the dog who was now having his ears rubbed by Catherine.

"That's my dog, Lucky. He follows me everywhere. Don't worry, he's very friendly."

Mary raised her eyebrows and gave the dog an unwelcoming glance.

Richard joined Catherine and was introduced to Lucky, who promptly rolled over on his back awaiting a belly rub. Richard obliged. Catherine looked over at Mary whose disgust was apparent. Richard straightened up and shook hands with William. "It's a fine day for your social, William, and that's a great dog you've got there."

"Oh yes, indeed he is. Quite a good watchdog too. Everyone is gathered out on the back lawn where it is quite shaded. Shall we go?"

Catherine sniffed the air. "I smell one of my favourite things I think - roast pig."

"You're right," William said, "two of them, in fact. Come this way," he said, leading them toward the archway entrance to the courtyard, Lucky walking close by Catherine and Richard.

Mary slipped her arm through William's. "I'm certain you won't mind helping me, William. I wouldn't want to turn my ankle before tonight's dance."

"What? No. I mean, yes. Er, by all means, lean on me. I shall ensure nothing happens to you." William placed his left hand over Mary's.

Richard raised his eyebrows and looked at Catherine quizzically. Catherine shrugged her shoulders, opened her eyes wide and shook her head.

"What was that all about?" Richard said quietly.

"I'm sure I don't know." Catherine slipped her arm through Richard's and in a falsetto tone continued, "I'm certain you won't mind helping me, Richard." She batted her eyes furiously. "I wouldn't want to turn my ankle before the dance tonight."

Catherine giggled and Richard suppressed his laughter by covering his mouth with his hand. He whispered, "You are a wicked girl, Catherine."

Smiling and chuckling, arm in arm, they followed a short distance behind William and Mary. Lucky saw a squirrel and darted away. Catherine and Richard laughed as they watched him race across the lawn.

A folly had been set up on the carefully manicured grass and under its shelter, tables were laden with fruit, sweetmeats and delicacies of every description. Beyond the edge of the grass, a path wound its way among the hedges and gardens which extended as far as the eye could see. To one side of the grassy section were sandy areas on which the spits had been erected to roast a large steer and the pigs Catherine's nose had detected.

"Come Mary, you must meet my parents," William said, nodding toward his left.

"Delighted."

"We must also greet our congenial hosts," Catherine said to Richard.

The foursome made their way through the many people standing in groups talking and nibbling on the refreshments.

The Earl and Countess of Fotheringham were seated in a shady alcove of the mansion. The Countess smiled broadly as the young people approached.

"Catherine, how delightful to see you again, and you, Richard." The Countess looked up at them and nodded, her white face and gray hair melding into one in the shadows.

"Our pleasure, Lady Harrison, I'm sure. Thank you for inviting us to this obviously wonderful feast," Catherine said, with a slight curtsey. "Lord Harrison, always a pleasure to see you," she continued.

"What, what? Oh, it's you, Catherine. Nice to see you again," he said loudly.

Richard looked at the Earl and decided Catherine's description of him was quite accurate, right down to his portly belly and pointy ears. "I'm happy to meet you at last, Lord Harrison," he said. "Richard Pedley here. I did some work for the Countess." The grunt that followed from the Earl was right in keeping with the rest of him.

Mary was surprised, and ultimately pleased, to find William's parents were quite old. He must have been a surprise to them, she thought.

"Mother, father, I'd like you to meet Mary Ainsworth, Catherine's cousin, the young lady I was telling you about."

"What did he say, Eleanor? Speak up, William," Lord Harrison said in a booming voice. "Who is this?"

Eleanor leaned closer to her husband, "It's William's friend, Mary Ainsworth, you know, the girl he was telling us about the other day."

"Oh yes, yes. So very nice to meet you, Mary. I see William has not exaggerated your beauty," Lord Harrison said, approvingly.

Mary blushed. "You are too kind, Lord Harrison. But I pale in comparison to your wife, the beautiful Lady Harrison." Mary looked from one to the other.

"I am flattered, young lady, but I'm much too old to be called beautiful; no matter your intentions, Mary, I thank you. It's not often compliments come my way anymore," Lady Harrison said.

"Not flattery, Lady Harrison. Just the simple truth," Mary said. In fact, it was not a lie, as Eleanor Harrison had been a beauty in her youth and despite the passing of years, most of her good looks were still visible. There was such a contrast in appearance between her and her rather ugly husband, Mary wondered why she had married him.

"What'd she say? Speak up, girl."

"Mary was just complimenting us, Edward," Lady Eleanor said.

"Very nice, very nice. Glad to hear it."

"My father's a little deaf," William said, unnecessarily.

"It's a lovely day today and you young people must be hungry. Go help yourselves over there," William's mother said, waving an elegant hand toward the heavily laden tables.

"A splendid idea," William said, tucking Mary's arm under his.

"Perhaps we'll have the opportunity to talk to you later, Richard," Lady Harrison said. "I have an idea about something I'd like you to make for us."

"Whenever you wish, Lady Harrison. I am at your service."

They were barely out of earshot, when Edward Harrison turned his head to his wife and said, "I'm very happy to see William with a young woman, Eleanor. Given that he has ever only brought home male friends, I was very much afraid we would never have grandchildren, if you know what I mean."

Eleanor placed her hand on one side of her mouth. "It appears to me William is quite smitten with the young lady. I hope he doesn't get his heart broken."

"Why would he?"

"Because she is very beautiful and William is ..." Eleanor twisted her mouth.

The Earl looked toward the food tables and rubbed his rumbling stomach. "What? William is a fine young man any woman would be happy to have."

Eleanor sighed as she looked at her husband and at the back of her retreating son. How unfortunate William looks like his father's side of the family rather than mine. Her reverie was broken by the arrival of another group of friends.

Richard and Catherine reached the tables before Mary and William, as the latter kept stopping to introduce Mary to many of the guests.

Richard observed them quizzically. "William certainly seems enamoured of your cousin, Catherine."

"I know. He's been besotted since the first day. What I don't understand is how or why Mary's aversion to him changed so suddenly. She was nasty to him and now ... I mean, she is positively smothering him with a cloak of enchantment and enticing smiles." Catherine shook her head.

Richard smiled. "She certainly appears to be infatuated by him. There is no accounting for what attracts one person to another."

"It's a mystery to me, but I'm not going to worry about it. Have a date," she said, holding one up in front of Richard's mouth. "Delicious. And look at all these sweets," Catherine said, closing her eyes in exaggerated ecstasy as she savoured a chocolate concoction.

"If you keep popping those in your mouth that fast, you will grow to the size of a mountain," Richard said, laughing.

"Piffle!" Catherine took another and looked around the crowd. "Where are Mary and William now? They've disappeared."

"I'm sure I don't know. I was too busy watching a beautiful lady eating sweets."

"Humphf," Catherine said through a mouthful of chocolate.

Having noticed no gardens visible from where they stood, and wanting to get William on his own, Mary had expressed a great interest in flowers and the area William had mentioned previously, so at that moment, he was showing her through a vast garden on the far side of the right wing of the house. They were wending their way slowly through the twisting paths, Mary clinging to him as if she were in danger of falling off a cliff.

"Not all the flowers are in bloom now, Mary, and you must come see it in the summertime. If you choose to walk all the way to the centre, there is a beautiful fountain, with benches where we can sit," William said. His body seemed to quiver with excitement, his hand and arm movements were jerky and uncoordinated.

"I'd be happy to walk there, if you would want to," Mary said, demurely, looking up at him from under her lashes, quite an accomplishment as she was only a couple of inches shorter than he, thanks to her new shoes.

As promised, the fountain was large and very beautiful. There were benches at intervals around the wall which contained the water. In the centre stood a tall, graceful lady, her gaze following the line of an upraised arm pointing to a far-off place in the sky, while in her other arm, she held a large urn from which poured a steady stream of gurgling water. Carved into the base of the statue were birds who would never sing and flowers whose blooms would never die.

As Mary trailed her hand in the water, several interested fish swam over. "Oh!" she exclaimed, withdrawing her hand quickly. "You have fish in here. I need a cloth."

William swiftly produced a silk handkerchief and offered it to her. "Don't worry - they don't bite."

Mary pulled her mouth into a tight line to stop herself from saying she didn't want smelly fish touching her hand. As William reached to take the silk cloth from her, Mary grasped his arm and pulled him toward her. "Please sit down beside me, William. I like to be near to you."

William obliged, nearly tipping backwards into the fountain in his eagerness.

"I don't quite know how to say this," Mary said, lowering her head, "because I've never felt this way before, but I ..." Her words were cut off by a loud bark as Lucky came racing up to them.

"What's the matter, boy? Did you miss us?" William rubbed the dog's head vigorously. "We really should take him back to the party, Mary, in case he damages the flowers. I can also show you my herb garden, if you wish. It's quite large and smells wonderful, even now."

Mary gave the dog a nasty look. She did not appreciate having her speech interrupted, but she put a smile on her face before replying.

"Anything you wish," Mary said agreeably, secretly wondering if she would manage to conceal her disinterest for very much longer.

They had been looking at the plants for only a short time before Mary had to stifle a yawn while William was in the midst of explaining the properties of assorted herbs. Lucky had disappeared whether out of boredom or to follow his nose back to the food.

The sun began to wane and long shadows were making their way across the greenery when Mary pointedly remarked, "The sun goes down so early these days. I'm afraid I'm getting a chill." She shivered slightly.

"Oh I'm so sorry. How thoughtless of me keeping you out here this long. Let me give you my jacket."

"I wouldn't think of having you remove your lovely jacket, William, when you look so elegant. Besides, I wouldn't want you to get a chill. Perhaps your arm around my shoulders would suffice."

William blushed but obliged hastily, pulling Mary against his side. "Is that better?"

"Much, thank you." She snuggled closer.

By the time they arrived back at the grassy area, a huge fire was going and most of the gentry had gone into the house, making way for the local villagers who were now eating and making merry. Lucky's earlier departure was now explained as he was busy begging for tidbits. He came running when he spotted his master and to Mary's chagrin, William removed his arm to pet the dog.

"I'm cold and it looks like the cool air caused many of the guests to go inside," Mary said.

"Oh dear," William said, replacing his arm hastily. "We'll go right in. It will soon be time to eat. This way, Mary." At the French doors, William instructed Lucky to stay outside. Seeing he was being left behind, Lucky raced back to see if he could cadge any more food.

The air was warm and the lights bright inside the large great room where everyone had gathered. Mary and William joined his parents just as dinner was announced. They all walked in together and Mary was asked to sit at the Earl's right hand. William sat on his mother's left, opposite Mary. She tried not to show her amazement at the variety of food presented in each of several courses, although she found she couldn't eat a great deal. William expressed his concern over her lack of appetite, but Mary assured him that she just had a delicate constitution, which seemed to increase, rather than assuage, his concern.

After dinner, they retired back to the great room which now held tables laden with wafers, sugar-spun anise, jellies and marmalades, along with candied fruits and spiced nuts. Spiced wine was served to aid the digestion, especially of those who had overindulged in the feast. When the music began in the ballroom, the guests drifted toward the merry sound.

Mary watched Richard and Catherine pass by Lucky, who was napping in the hall, and disappear through the doorway, but instead of following them, she turned to William. "William, I'm feeling a little faint. Is there somewhere I can go lie down?"

"Oh my dear. Shall I get Mother or one of the maids to attend to you? No doubt there is a guest bedroom available."

Lucky raised his head when he heard William's voice.

"No, no, no," Mary said hastily. "I don't want to trouble anyone. Your mother has to keep her guests entertained. Perhaps we could just retire to your chamber where I might sit for a few minutes."

"My chamber?" William croaked, then cleared his throat. "Uh, well, I don't know what to say. I mean, of course, I don't mind if you do, but what will anyone else think? I mean ..."

"Nonsense, William. Everyone knows you are an honourable man and would never do anything to disgrace your family. Besides, we won't be gone long."

"All right then. It's quite a distance, but if you're sure you can make it ..."

"I'm sure. Perhaps if I could just lean on you?"

"Certainly. Certainly." As Mary pressed into his chest, William could smell her heady perfume. His thoughts were swirling like the flickering light of the sconces, disturbed by their progress down a long corridor hung with paintings of his ancestors. Lucky followed quietly behind.

"Sorry it's such a long way," he said, as sounds of the music became fainter.

"That's quite all right, William. It just means we will have privacy."

Mary deliberately pulled his arm tighter, so he could feel the roundness of her bosom pressing on it. To divert his mind from the stirring in his groin, he began to relate anecdotes of the people in the paintings.

When they reached his quarters, Mary detached herself to enable William to light a lantern waiting on a stand by the door. She caught sight of Lucky. "Do you allow that dog to be in here?" she asked, allowing a modicum of annoyance to slip out.

"Oh yes. Lucky's no trouble. He always stays in my room while I'm here.

Behind William's back, Mary glowered at the dog. We'll see about that, she thought.

They entered a huge sitting room whose outer regions were barely visible in the single light. William hastened to his large desk and lit another which brought to life a sofa and assorted chairs, arranged in front of a fireplace whose grate had been laid with wood ready for lighting.

"Let me help you get settled on the sofa," William said.

Mary had no intention of lying on a sofa. "I really would prefer to lie down on a bed. I feel rather faint," Mary said, weaving slightly.

William reached for her in case she should fall and Mary quickly put her arms around his neck and sagged against him. He lifted her up in his arms. "Oh dear. If you can carry the lantern, I'll take you in and lay you on my bed," he said.

Mary took the light and they passed through the doorway into his bedroom, followed by Lucky who lay down near the fireplace. He watched his master and cocked his head when William didn't come and light the fire as usual. Mary set the lantern on a table, and William placed her gently on the bed. As he moved to step back, Mary kept her arms around him.

"Please stay with me. I need you."

"I ... I ... All right," he said, "but I'm afraid I'll fall on top of you if you don't let go."

"Would that be a bad thing?" Mary smiled seductively.

William looked at her for a moment, then bending to the pressure of her arms, gently placed his lips on hers. As he tried to pull away, she put her hand behind his neck and kissed him passionately. When Mary released him, he looked at her, somewhat dazed and confused.

"I thought you didn't feel well."

"I didn't, but I'm so much better now we're alone." She gazed at him sorrowfully. "Don't you like me, William?"

"LIKE you? Of course, I do. More, I love you, although it's much too soon to speak of that or to hope you could love me back."

I've won. Now to continue the deception. "Of course I love you, William. Can't you tell?"

William's heart raced. He was overwhelmed and speechless.

"Come. Lie down with me, so we can ... talk. Remove your jacket so you will be more comfortable."

He did as instructed and gingerly took his place, hands by his side, carefully maintaining a little distance between their bodies. It quickly became apparent to Mary she was going to have to give him a multitude of directions.

"Put your arm out here, so I might rest my head," she said turning toward him.

William did so and Mary cuddled up to him, placing her right arm on his chest before moving it up his neck to his face, where she stroked him lovingly. His arms moved of their own accord around her slim frame pulling her close. He felt the softness of her breasts pressing tightly against his chest.

Mary kissed him, then sat up. She had felt his arousal and looked down to make sure. His face turned red. "Can you unlace these ties?" she said indicating the front of her dress.

"I ... I suppose so." William sat up. His fingers fumbled with the ties, but eventually he succeeded in releasing her breasts from their constraints. He drew in a deep breath as he stared at the creamy roundness of her flesh, punctuated with erect nipples.

Mary smiled at him and gently pushed her breast toward him. "Wouldn't you like to touch this?" she asked seductively.

William tentatively put his hand on her breast and sighed. Instinct took over. He bent down, kissed the soft skin and ran his tongue around the nipple before taking it into his mouth and sucking on it. He groaned.

Mary's passions flared in spite of herself. She closed her eyes and pretended it was Donald now fondling and kissing her.

"It would be so much nicer if we removed our clothes, don't you think?"

William was shocked. "I ... I don't know. I suppose you're right." He stood, helped Mary up and they both began to disrobe. He gazed in awe and wonder at her naked body. "You ... you are so beautiful."

One look at William's organ told Mary he certainly wasn't Donald, but she determined not to care. As long as it worked, that was the main thing. She came close to him, pressing her mouth and body against his. He picked her up, laid her on the bed and immediately entered her, pumping up and down quickly. At the moment of climax, he threw his head back, yelled "Aaaaahhhh!" and rolled off her onto his back.

Mary was surprised, disgusted and frustrated all at once.

"Oh my darling! That was wonderful," he said. "I've never done this before."

I certainly didn't need you to tell me that. Aloud she said, "Neither have I." Suddenly, Mary started to cry.

"My darling," William said, gazing with concern into her crumpled face. "What's wrong?"

"I just realized we shouldn't ... shouldn't have ..." Her sobbing increased.

"What? I don't understand."

"We shouldn't have ... only married people are supposed to do that. I am so ashamed. I am disgraced." Mary buried her face in the pillow.

"Oh my dear. Oh. Please don't cry. I am so sorry. I didn't mean ... it's all my fault."

Mary's muffled cries continued.

"Please don't cry. I love you. What can I do to help?"

"Nothing. Nothing can help. It's too late. " Mary's cries increased.

William was at a loss. He had never even envisioned such a scenario taking place in his life. "There must be something."

Mary waited a moment to see if his brain would turn in the right direction, decided to give it a push. "This joy ..." she nearly choked on the word, "... is only for married people and we're not."

William's eyes opened wide as what she said finally registered. "I will marry you if you will have me. Mary?"

Mary raised her head slowly and snuffled. "Do you mean it? You really want to marry me?" she said, dabbing away the one tear she had managed to produce.

"Of course I do. We can get married next Spring and ..."

She raised her head and gazed at him mournfully. "I don't want to wait, William. If we don't get married till then, that means we won't be able to ... do this again. And I love you so much ... it would be such a hardship not being with you." She dropped back down on the pillow.

"Right. Well, um, what would you suggest?"

Mary sat up immediately. "Let's get married right away. I can't wait to have you hold me in your arms all night long. Besides, some other woman might come along and win your heart and I would be devastated." She stuck out her lower lip and gazed up under her lashes.

William blushed. "Never. I love you with my whole heart."

Mary smiled sweetly. "Then perhaps next week would be a good time? While everyone's here? I do need to have a gown made. We should tell your parents tonight."

"Next week??" William's mind was hardly able to keep up with all the unusual feelings he was experiencing.

"If you think that's too soon ..." Mary's face crumpled again and tears threatened to fall.

He gently put his hands on her face. "Don't cry my love. Next week will be perfectly fine."

Mary smiled. "I can hardly wait." She rose with alacrity and jumped out of bed. Lucky rose to his feet to watch. "I really find it disconcerting to have that dog looking at me," she said, grabbing up her clothes.

"Lucky's a good boy. He won't do anything. You'll get used to him."

We'll see about that, Mary thought, giving the dog a sour look.

They made their way back downstairs to find William's parents. The Earl and Countess of Fotheringham were sitting in the great room enjoying a spiced drink when the couple approached. They were, in turn, shocked, surprised and agreeable to the wedding of William and Mary.

It could safely be said the Earl in particular was delighted to know his son was marrying a woman, as he had believed secretly William had a preference for members of his own sex. So excited was Edward Harrison he stopped the music, asked for the guests' attention, announced the engagement of William and Mary and invited them all to return to Harrison Hall the following week to take part in the wedding of the happy couple. Shocked silence was followed immediately by clapping and a great deal of whispering.

It was late in the evening when Richard, Catherine and Mary stepped into the carriage to return to Hawkesbury Manor. Only sheer exhaustion kept Catherine from badgering Mary with a barrage of questions. To Richard's delight, she merely leaned her head on his shoulder and lightly slept. He smiled as he brushed some loose hair back from her face.

Chapter 18

Hawkesbury Manor, Late September 1587

The next morning at breakfast, Catherine was disappointed, though not surprised, that Mary did not show up.

"Richard, tell me I'm not dreaming. I really did hear the Earl say Mary and William were getting married?"

"You're not dreaming. I heard it too. Are you really surprised?"

"Surprised is an understatement. I am totally baffled because Mary always told me she couldn't stand William and adamantly refused to go riding with me in case we met him somewhere along the way. And now she's going to marry him! Next week! I swear I will never understand that girl." Catherine chomped down on a sausage to emphasize her amazement.

"It just proves you never know where the heart will take you, Catherine. I know where mine has taken me, and I hope someday yours will meet me there."

Catherine looked quizzically at Richard. "What do you mean?"

"Nothing, Cathy. It's just love is in the air, I guess," Richard said as he swung his fork in the air. "After all, we both hope to fall in love and get married someday, don't we?"

"I suppose." Catherine gazed off into space. "But I want to have adventures. There is so much to see and do in other parts of the world."

"There is no reason why a person can't do both. After all, it is married people with families who will settle the New World. So it is quite ..."

Richard's speech was interrupted by the entrance of Mary.

"Here you are at last! Good morning, Mary. You're looking a little pale. I guess all the excitement last night was too much for you. Did you not sleep well?" Catherine said.

"I think something I ate disagreed with me," Mary said, sitting down.

"Oh, that's too bad. Nothing ever upsets my stomach. I'm dying to hear all about your engagement. When did William propose? Did you know he was going to ask you? I thought you didn't like him. What made you change your mind? Have you been having secret lover trysts? Do you have a dress already?"

Mary stared at her cousin and helped herself to some food instead of answering.

"Perhaps you should confine yourself to one question at a time, Catherine," said Richard. "You do tend to be a bit overwhelming."

"Sorry. Pick one or two and give me the answers, Mary."

Mary put some meat in her mouth before replying. "No, I don't have a dress yet, but Lady Harrison is having her seamstress make one for me. I will be having a fitting today," she said, reaching for a scone.

"Ooooh, you have a ring!" Catherine squealed, leaning over and grasping Mary's right hand.

"Yes, it's an heirloom in William's family given by the firstborn son to his betrothed." Framed by an intricate design of gold filigree were brilliant emeralds surrounding a huge Marquise diamond.

"Oooh! It is beautiful, Mary!"

"Thank you."

"But this is so sudden. How ..."

"I know. William proposed last night and absolutely insisted we get married right away. He said his heart would be broken if we had to delay the wedding. The Earl has persuaded the minister to accept a Marriage Bond, so instead of waiting three weeks for the readings, we will be married next Sunday, immediately after the reading takes place. We are signing the contract today."

"How very exciting. But what made you change your mind about William? You always gave me to understand you didn't like him."

"Nonsense! I never said any such thing. I think he's very nice. Besides, when the poor boy poured his heart out to me telling me how much he loved me and couldn't stand to be away from me, what else could I do?"

"What did your mother say?" Richard asked.

"She was a little flustered at first, but then mother gets that way for no reason at all. She is quite happy for me, although wondering how she will deal with Father."

"Will he come for the wedding?"

"I think not. Time and distance won't allow him to get here," Mary said.

"But ..." Catherine began.

"I really don't think I can eat any more," Mary said, pushing her plate away.

"Good heavens! You hardly ate anything. You will fade away to a shadow if you keep that up."

"I don't think there is any fear of that. I must finish getting ready before William comes to pick me up. I won't be around much this week as there are too many things to do at Harrison Hall. Oh, I almost forgot. You will be my bridesmaid, Catherine. If you will, of course," she added as an afterthought.

"I would be delighted. But what shall I wear?"

"Whatever you have on hand. Don't worry about it. I am the one, after all, at whom people will be looking. I'm sure you have something suitable."

"I suppose I do."

"Then it's settled. And don't concern yourself about the flowers. William's mother has insisted on taking care of those. I'll see you later." Mary quickly exited the room.

"There you have it, Cathy. True love surmounts all obstacles."

"Nonsense! Telling me she never said anything against William. As if I would make up such a thing," Catherine said indignantly.

"No need to worry your pretty little head about it, Cathy. The die is cast."

Catherine drummed her fingers on the table. "Now I shall have to think about what to wear." She sighed.

"Whatever you choose, you will be the prettiest girl there."

"What nonsense you talk."

"It's true. You are a very beautiful young woman, Catherine."

Catherine blushed. "Really! What has come over you Richard?!" She chewed and thought for a moment. "Oh! I know. I have a dress I brought back from Italy. I think that will work quite nicely."

"There you are. The problem is solved."

"I'm glad I don't have any others. But this whole marriage thing still confuses me. I just don't understand ..."

"Let it be, Catherine.   Perhaps it's time to think about your own future and what you want to do with it."

"That's such a bother. Can't I just let it happen?"

Richard laughed. "You could, of course, but I think you would find it much more to your liking if you made some plans which would include where you would like to go and with whom, what you really want to do, where you want to live - things like that." He stared at her intently. "Think about it Cathy. You should make the most of the many years you have to live on this earth and not just let them slip away into oblivion. Wouldn't you like to end up as an old lady who looks back on her life with a great deal of satisfaction, knowing she has accomplished most, if not all, of the dreams she had as a young woman, rather than someone who says 'if only I had done so and so'? 'If only' is a very sad expression, Cathy."

"I do not want to be an old lady at all!"

Richard laughed again. "You mean you want to die young?"

"No, of course not. I mean, I just want to stay young forever."

"I think that's possible, Cathy, if your heart and attitude remain young, which, in my opinion, will happen if you live a fulfilling life, doing the things that make you happy ... with a person who makes you happy. I certainly intend to try."

Catherine was silent for a few minutes, thoughtfully chewing her food.   She looked directly at Richard. "What is it you want to do, Richard?"

"I want to go to the New World, find some land and build my own home. I want to help settle that country with my wife and hopefully some children."

Catherine's mouth fell open. "Your WIFE?! Are you getting married?"

Richard laughed at the expression on her face. "I haven't asked her yet, but I'm hoping she'll say yes."

Catherine was agog, food forgotten. "Who is it? Someone I know?"

"Indeed, she is." Richard said.

"Who?"

"I don't think I'll tell you just yet." Richard smiled wickedly, knowing how Catherine would be dying to hear all the details. "And now I must get to work. Lady Harrison has ordered a special table she wants to use for displaying some ornament." Richard headed to the door. "I'll see you later, Cathy."

"Wait! WAIT! You must tell me who this person is. I shall explode with curiosity if you don't tell me."

Richard laughed heartily. "You think about it and see if you can guess. Tell me later."

Catherine dropped her knife on the table. "You are mean, Richard Pedley!" she called after his retreating back. His laughter echoed from the hall. "Oooh! That makes me mad!" She toyed with the food on her plate, finally picking up a piece of bread and heading outside toward the pond.

She tossed the bread into the water and watched while Mr. Getaway and a couple of his friends pulled it apart, opening their mouths and swallowing their treat. When the flurry of marine activity had subsided, Catherine went to the summerhouse, flopped down on the bench, leaned her elbows on her knees and cupped her chin with her hand. She was disturbed by the thought that Richard had a woman to whom he was going to propose marriage, and at a loss to understand her feelings of disappointment and regret.

She sat up straight as it suddenly occurred to her she would be very lonely and upset if Richard were to go away. *I would miss him dreadfully. What would I do without him?* She started to cry. *He is my friend. I love him.* Her eyes opened wide at the last thought. *Could that be the answer? I love him?* Catherine's tears stopped. Her mind was awhirl. *He loves me! That explains perfectly what he was talking about. And I love him. He cannot ask someone else to* marry him. He cannot! I must figure out a way to make him see that. She jumped to her feet. Why does life have to be so complicated?

Chapter 19

Harrison Hall, October 1587

The week passed quickly in a flurry of activity.

Richard paced back and forth at the foot of the stairs waiting for Catherine to appear. At a rustle behind him, he turned around. "It's about ..." His voice trailed away and he stood gazing at her.

"What's the matter? Don't you like it?" Catherine said, touching the lace shawl which hung over the blue and ivory silk gown.

"Catherine ... you have taken my breath away. You look absolutely gorgeous. The beauty of the heavens above pales by comparison." Richard extended his hand to help her down the last two steps. "I hardly recognized you. Oh, the bride is going to be so jealous."

Catherine blushed. "You do talk nonsense, Richard. But thank you."

"It's most assuredly not nonsense." Richard bent low and kissed her hand. "Come this way, princess. Your coach awaits you."

Catherine laughed. "What a silly, you are."

The church was full when they arrived and joined Mary in the vestibule. Mary's face turned sour when she looked at Catherine. "I thought you were going to get a dress out of your wardrobe," she said.

"But I did. This is one I brought back from Italy last year. Don't you like it?"

"I think it's inappropriate, not to mention the colour doesn't suit you. Never mind. Can't be helped now." Mary turned and walked to a table to retrieve her garland of roses and rosemary.

Catherine looked stricken. She turned her eyes, now beginning to tear up, to Richard. He was scowling.

"Don't give that witch the satisfaction of seeing you cry. You look beautiful and she is jealous. Come on now, smile." He carefully wiped an errant tear that had escaped.

Catherine cleared her throat, lifted her chin and gave a half smile to Richard. "You are always so kind, Richard," she said softly.

He smiled back. "I must go and take my seat now." He kissed her lightly on the cheek. Catherine's eyes watched him lovingly as he walked away.

The service was short and people wasted no time getting outside where the air was cool but pleasant after the stuffiness of the church. The chatter was lively among those waiting for their coaches to take them back to Harrison Hall, much of it speculation on the speed of the wedding.

"Oh, look at all the flowers," Catherine exclaimed, as she and Richard stepped from their coach in front of the manor. "How gorgeous!"

Richard looked appreciatively at the garlands of yellow chrysanthemums, interwoven with colourful leaves, which were strung across the entranceway and all the windows of the manor.

"Very beautiful, indeed."

"Let's hurry and see what they've done in the courtyard." Catherine fairly dragged Richard through the arch.

"Catherine, slow down. You're dressed like an elegant lady and must walk like one."

"Phooey!" she said, but did slow her pace.

Embankments of flowers surrounded a large section of the courtyard, and in their midst, musicians were playing, while the guests stood around drinking the popular warm, spiced wine. As

Catherine looked at the fashionable outfits of the other ladies, she became a little dubious about the dress she had chosen.

"The ladies are certainly attired in the latest fashion," she said, her voice tinged with a little regret. "I'm thinking mine is somewhat out-of-date."

"I'm no expert on fashion, Catherine, but I do know you out-shine every woman here." Richard smiled and raised his wine in a toast to her.

She smiled and, having determined to speak privately to him, slowly moved away from the ever-increasing throng of people, Richard falling into step beside her. When they were finally in a clear space, Catherine turned to her companion. "There's something I want to talk to you about, Richard, but I'm not quite sure how to begin."

"What is it? You know you can talk to me about anything." He looked at her with interest.

Nerves were getting the better of her and Catherine drew in a deep breath. "Last week, you said something about asking someone to marry you. Have you done that yet?" She held her breath, waiting for his reply.

"No. No, I haven't. Why?"

Catherine sighed in relief. "I know it's none of my business, but I don't think you should ask her."

Richard's eyes opened wide and his eyebrows raised in surprise. "Really? And why is that?"

Catherine looked off into space. "Because she's not the right person for you."

Richard smiled. "And how would you know that?"

"Because ... because ... I am," she mumbled, still not looking at him.

"What did you say?"

"Nothing." Catherine said, regretting her decision to speak. She looked over at the crowd and made a move to leave. "I think they're going inside to eat now."

Richard took hold of her arm. "Catherine, wait. Look at me."

She turned around, but kept her eyes on the ground.

"You said 'I am', didn't you?"

Catherine continued to hang her head without responding. Richard gently lifted up her chin, but she still wouldn't meet his gaze.

"Catherine? Look at me. Did you not guess you were the lady of whom I spoke?"

She looked up at him with wide eyes.

"I have loved you forever, Catherine, and I hoped you would love me in return. I've been waiting a long time for some kind of sign from you." He continued looking at her, smiled and then laughed. "Are you going to speak or just stand there staring at me with your mouth hanging open?"

Catherine found her voice. "Me? You were talking about me?"

"Who else would I be talking about?"

"I don't know." A mix of relief and happiness flooded her being. "But why didn't you say so? And my mouth was not hanging open!" She hit him softly on the arm.

"Because you weren't ready to hear it. I needed you to come to the conclusion on your own - and yes it was." Richard smiled and took both her hands. "My darling, I have loved you for as long as I can remember. I want to marry you and spend the rest of my life with you."

Catherine's heart beat faster, her joy lighting up her face. "I love you too, Richard."

He pulled her close in a loving embrace but, conscious of their surroundings, let her go quickly.. "We will do nothing, of course, until Jeremy comes home. I will have to ask his blessing."

"Oh. I wish we didn't have to wait, but you are right. I think Jeremy will be very happy, don't you?"

"I certainly hope so. I also hope you were serious when you said you wanted to travel and live in Virginia or somewhere in the new lands, because that is my dream."

"I was. I am. Oh, Richard, what a wonderful life we will have together." Catherine was nearly jumping with excitement, her mind awhirl. "When should I start planning our wedding?"

"Not until Jeremy comes back, because there is always the possibility he might object."

"He won't. He wouldn't dare!"

Richard chuckled. "If he sees that look on your face, I agree. It would be enough to quell the objection of any man." Richard laughed aloud. "We must keep this a secret for now, Catherine, pending Jeremy's return."

"UGH! I want to tell the world!"

"So do I, but ... patience, my dear. Patience."

"All right, my love. I'll do my best. But it's not going to be easy. And I am going to plan our wedding because I just know Jeremy will be happy for us, so don't try and stop me," Catherine said emphatically.

"Try to stop a whirlwind?? I wouldn't dream of it." Richard smiled broadly. "Now I think we must go and offer congratulations to the newlyweds."

"Not to mention getting something to eat. I am positively starving!"

Catherine linked her arm in Richard's as they headed toward the door with the rest of the guests.

Richard smiled at her. "Remember, not a word. And try not to look so happy. Your face will give it all away."

"Is this better?" she said, pulling her mouth down and looking up at him with hangdog eyes.

Richard burst out laughing. "You are impossible, Catherine. Utterly impossible."

Chapter 20

The Crown & Anchor, Late 1587

Unaware of anything happening back at Hawkesbury Manor, Jeremy was enjoying his life with Meggie and her family. When he thought periodically about his home, he would feel momentary pangs of guilt, but these were easily assuaged when Meggie appeared. Days had turned into weeks, and Jeremy had to keep reminding himself that he was there for a purpose, although he was beginning to wonder if he were on a fool's errand as very little information had been exchanged by the seedier patrons of the inn.

Meggie's happiness showed in her lightness of step and singing as she went about her chores and had not gone unnoticed by her mother. Nancy brought this to her husband's attention while he was wiping down the tables, but he told her she was imagining it.

"Ian McIntosh, you're as blind as old Billy McWhirtle. Ye cannot see what is right before your eyes. I be thinking I know the cause of her happiness too."

"And what might that be - in your imagination, that is?"

"I think she's in love with yon Thomas Smithson."

"Don't be daft, woman. She doesn't know anything about him."

"Don't be daft yerself, Mr. McIntosh! I've got eyes in me head and I see what I see. Not that I mind. I think Thomas is a fine young man, somewhere under that awful beard."

"I agree with you there. I quite like the lad. But we don't know anything about him, so how can we know he would be good for our Meggie - if she liked him, which I'm not convinced she does, at least not in the way you mean."

"Ach, there's no fool like an old fool. Open your eyes the next time the two of them are together, and you'll see for yourself, Ian. As a matter of fact, I think they're out checking for leftovers in the garden. Go take a look."

Ian sighed audibly and handed his wife the cloth he had been using. "If you won't let me get my work done in peace, ye may as well help me out."

"Just don't be all day about it then. Take a look and come back."

Ian left the room shaking his head and wondering if his wife was going to start imagining anything else. When he reached the kitchen window, he saw Jeremy and Meggie laughing together and pointing at some trees which marked the end of the garden. To his astonishment, he watched Meggie lean down and kiss Jeremy on the forehead. "Well, well," he said aloud. "Well, well."

He trudged back to the main room of the inn.

"So. Did you see them?" Nancy asked as soon as he came in.

"Yes. They were looking at something in the trees."

"And ...?"

"And that's it. They just looked happy, that's all. That's what it looked like to me."

"Ach, ye are a fair daft man," Nancy said. "Here's your cloth. Finish the job yourself. I've got me own work to do." She left the room in a flurry of skirts.

At least I don't have to worry about her imagining things. My Nancy's got a sharp eye. Never in a million years would Ian admit to his wife that he was wrong about anything.

Chapter 21

Hawkesbury Manor, Early December 1587

When Mary announced the news of her pregnancy to William in late November, he was ecstatic and lost no time in informing his parents of the coming arrival. Knowing little about female anatomy or details about pregnancy, William believed her when she said she had become pregnant on the first night they were together.

Mary made the most of her 'delicate' condition, getting William to wait on her and making sure he understood that the lack of sex was his own fault for having caused her to become pregnant. She said that the birth would likely occur in July, although she knew perfectly well that it would be a few months before that.

Annabelle had happily returned to her own home after the wedding, and with Mary gone, Catherine found the house surprisingly quiet and time weighing heavily. When she saw Mary's coach approaching, Catherine welcomed the interruption to her daily routine, hoping it would chase away what she called her pre-Christmas doldrums.

As they sat across from each other in the sitting-room waiting for tea, Catherine noticed that Mary seemed rather pale, but, out of politeness, refrained from mentioning it. "It's very nice of you to call, Mary. We haven't seen much of you since your wedding."

"William and I have been rather busy changing things around in the manor to suit ourselves, and getting ready for the Christmas festivities. We are having a big celebration for Twelfth Night and a great many of the royalty will be there. The cooks are baking no end of goodies. Oh." Mary hesitated. "If you think you would be comfortable, you and Richard could join us, if you don't already have plans."

It was rather apparent to Catherine that they were an after-thought. Did Mary really think they would not be 'comfortable' around royalty? She unconsciously raised an eyebrow as she mulled over Mary's words. "How nice of you to invite us. We'd be delighted to come."

The sarcastic tone was completely lost on Mary, who was look-ing around the room distractedly. Catherine decided to change the subject. "How are you enjoying your married life? Is William being kind to you?"

"Kind? Oh yes, I suppose so, but he's an absolute bore. I avoid his company whenever possible, although he tends to stick to me like a leech."

Catherine raised her eyebrows. This wasn't how she expected married people to behave. "It's still a mystery to me why you married him. I was quite sure you didn't care for him."

A maid arrived carrying a tea tray which she set up between the girls. Catherine said she would do the serving and the young girl left.

Mary chose to ignore Catherine's previous comment. "Enough about William. I came to tell you my news," she said. "I'm with child."

Catherine clapped her hands. "How wonderful! Congratulations! You must be terribly excited."

"Not really. It just means several months of carrying extra weight around, not to mention feeling rather sick most of the time. William, of course, is tremendously happy. He thinks he's done something marvellous. Stupid fool!"

Catherine was somewhat taken aback. "I daresay most fathers feel like that. Meaning no disrespect to your choice of a husband, I must admit I hope for your sake and the child's, that he or she looks like you and not William."

"It won't look like William."

"Hopefully not, but one can't really be certain."

"I can."

Catherine looked puzzled. Mary regarded Catherine thought-fully as she debated whether it would be advantageous to tell her version of the truth. Deciding it would be, she said, "Can you keep a secret?"

"Uh, yes."

"The baby won't look like William because he isn't the father - thank goodness."

Catherine's mouth fell open. "Not ... the father? But who ...?"

Mary sighed. "Through no fault of my own, I found myself in the terrible position of being pregnant and unable to marry the man responsible. That is why I turned to William because I knew he loved me and would agree to marry."

Catherine rose, went to Mary, knelt and took her hand. "You should have told us, Mary. We would have made the father marry you."

"You misunderstand. I did not wish to marry him. He is too far below my station."

"But who is he?"

"I'm surprised you cannot guess."

"I really have no idea."

"Promise that you will not say or do anything to let him know that I've told you."

"Yes. All right."

Mary pulled her hand away and half covered her face. "Donald is the father. He fell madly in love with me and became very ardent in his pursuit of my affections. Of course, I spurned his advances, but one day, he caught me at a moment when I was feeling homesick and I foolishly gave in to his desires." She snuffled against her fingers. "Afterwards, I was disgusted with myself and the whole business and determined to put it out of my mind. It didn't occur to me that I might have become pregnant, as it happened only once, and really against my will."

Catherine jumped to her feet. "How very dreadful of him to take advantage of you like that! He should be punished. I will speak to Richard."

"No, no," Mary said quickly. "You promised not to say or do anything. Donald has no idea the child is his and no one else must ever know. I expect you to honour your word."

Catherine pulled a sour face. "I will keep my word." She flopped into her chair.

"However, now you appreciate why I said he would be most unsuitable for my husband."

"Yes, I see." Catherine's mind was racing. "Does William know?"

"Of course not! When the time comes, I shall say the baby has arrived early. William believes everything I tell him."

"You are fortunate then, although I'm sure he will wonder." It occurred to Catherine that William would not be the only one wondering.

"Perhaps." Mary groaned and placed a hand on her stomach.

"Are you all right?" Catherine asked anxiously, looking at Mary's pale face.

"I ... I'm not sure. I feel strange. Perhaps I'd better be going."

Mary stood up and swayed slightly. Catherine jumped to her feet and grabbed her. "You cannot leave feeling like this. Come and lie down in your old room."

The girls slowly made their way upstairs, with Mary clutching tightly to Catherine's arm.

"Let me get you out of those heavy clothes," Catherine said.

By the time only her shift remained, Mary was swaying on her feet. Catherine hurriedly helped her lie down and gently placed the covers over her. Mary's breathing quickened.

"I think something's happening. It doesn't feel right. Oh God! I feel … liquid. Catherine, help me!" She clutched at Catherine's sleeve.

Catherine panicked. "Mary! Wait, wait! I'll get Mrs. Stewart. She'll know what to do. Don't worry. I'll be right back." She raced from the room.

A few minutes later, Catherine, Mrs. Stewart and one of the serving-girls from the kitchen arrived, carrying rags, towels, a basin and hot water. Mary looked was visibly upset and very pale.

"Please help me. I'm frightened," she said, her eyes pleading.

Mrs. Stewart patted Mary's hand. "Don't worry, you'll be fine. Martha, away you go to the kitchen and keep an eye on things till I get back."

The serving-girl left hurriedly. Mrs. Stewart carefully lifted the covers. Catherine gasped when she saw the blood-stained garment. Mrs. Stewart, placed the basin under Mary and wiped the blood off her body.

"What's wrong?" Mary said.

"Catherine told me you're pregnant and I'm afraid you're losing the baby, miss. It happens sometimes, but not to worry, you'll be able to have plenty more. How far along are you?"

"We were married at the beginning of October, so coming up to two or three months, I guess. Ooof!"

"There. It's done, miss." Mrs. Stewart looked at the basin. "You were more than that, miss. This one is nearer four months."

"You're mistaken. I'm telling you it's only been since the beginning of October." Mary managed to put authority into her voice, despite her pain.

Mrs. Stewart raised her eyebrows and looked at Catherine, who said, "Two or three months, Mrs. Stewart."

The older woman looked at the two girls and wisely decided to hold her tongue on the subject. "You'll be fine in a couple of days, miss." After she finished washing and cleaning up, Mrs. Stewart left the girls alone.

"Will Mrs. Stewart keep this to herself?"

"Yes, she is not a gossip and knows when not to say anything," Catherine said. "I had better send someone over to Harrison Hall to let William know." She made to leave.

"Yes, but there's no hurry. William will just come rushing over here making a big fuss. I'd rather just sleep for a while before you let them know."

Catherine was dubious but didn't want to argue with Mary under the circumstances. "Of course. You must be exhausted. Pull the cord when you wake up and we'll get you something to eat."

"Thank you." Mary closed her eyes and Catherine quietly left the room.

Catherine sat in the living-room thinking about the morning's happenings and what Mary had told her about Donald. Could Mary's story be true? Had Donald really taken advantage of her? The more she thought about the whole situation, the more Catherine decided that Mary was lying. I know she didn't like William. That was just too obvious, plus I saw her making eyes at Donald and always insisting that he be the one who help her off the horse. Who knows what else she may have done.

Her promise to keep silent about the situation seemed irrelevant now that Mary had lost the baby, but Catherine decided that she would talk it over with Richard to get his opinion.

Chapter 22

The Crown & Anchor, Christmas 1587

Jeremy was very surprised to discover the McIntoshes served a big meal at Christmas time for the families of their regular customers. He was determined to help out in the only way he could - financially. He told Nancy he would buy not only the usual turkeys, but would purchase a wild boar, which a local hunter had assured him he would kill and deliver ahead of the date. As boars were usually served only in the homes of the wealthy, Jeremy said he would be happy to tell her how to cook it. He refrained, however, from suggesting that the boar's head be used for a table decoration.

Early December found the inn filled with the tantalizing aroma of Christmas puddings and mince pies. Between keeping up the daily meals and preparing all the extras for the special dinner, the kitchen was a flurry of activity all day. Jeremy was pressed into service in the early part of the day, mixing ingredients for the different dishes and assorted other jobs that he could do while sitting down. He had little time for missing his own family Christmas, and indeed, felt right at home where he was.

December 24th was the day of the big dinner, and the inn was bursting at the seams with children and adults talking and laughing.

The spicy smell of a huge Wassail bowl dominated the air around the bar where it sat for the enjoyment of the adults.

Those who could play the fiddle did so, and in the little space available, many of the others danced, cheered on by the watchers. In between the dancing, someone started singing a Christmas carol and everyone joined in. The festivities lasted for three hours, at the end of which time, everyone heartily sang 'We Wish You a Merry Christmas', the signal the celebration was over. Children were given little sweetmeats to take home. Hugs, good wishes and a multitude of thanks were given to the hosts when the guests were departing.

After the last family had left, Nancy collapsed in a chair. "Faith, I'm just plain tuckered out," she said.

"But it was a wonderful evening," Meggie said, "and tomorrow you can rest. I'm quite sure there's enough food left over so no cooking will be required."

"I must say that boar was really tasty, Thomas," Ian said, rubbing his belly. "First time I ever ate it. Thank ye for providing it."

"I'm sure you're most welcome, Ian. I can't recall ever having this much fun at Christmas time. What an absolutely fantastic evening!"

"Why don't you and father go to bed, Mum. Thomas and I will do the washing up," Meggie said.

"Sounds like a good plan to me," said Ian, standing up and turning toward the door.

"A good plan, but we will make sure everything is cleared up out of here," said Nancy. "Come, Mr. McIntosh, ye're not getting out of work that easily."

Thomas sighed, but didn't argue. As her parents carried dishes and leftovers to the kitchen, Meggie started washing. Jeremy sat in a chair beside her, towel in hand. She smiled at him and he winked back.

"Are you happy now, Mrs.?" Ian said. "The place is fair cleaned up and wiped down now."

"Aye. Looks like you've done a good job, Ian, although a bit on the slow side. Ye must be getting old." Nancy laughed at the indignant look on his face.

"Not so old that I can't chase you up the stairs," Ian retorted, making a dash toward her.

"Oh, ye're an awful man, coming after me like that when I've been working like a drudge for the last month. Away with ye. And talking like that in front of the children. Have ye no shame, man?!" Her big smile belied her words.

Meggie and Jeremy laughed as the older couple continued bantering while climbing the stairs to their rooms.

"They really love each other, don't they?" Jeremy said.

"Yes, they do, Thomas. They have a wonderful relationship, with never a harsh word because each knows that love is always present no matter what. It's the sort of marriage I want."

Jeremy stopped wiping a dish. "Oh, Meggie. We have that love, don't you think? I know I would never hurt you and will always take care of you. You are my heart, my soul, my life."

"This is a fine time to be telling me the likes of that, when I'm up to my elbows in soap and water and can't make any kind of affectionate response!"

"Really! Well, if you're going to let a little soapy water come between us, what hope have we for ..."

"It's like that, is it? Take this then." Meggie leaned down, gently slapped her wet hands on either side of Jeremy's face, then swiftly put her arms around his neck and kissed him soundly. "How does that suit your lordship," she said, starting to draw back.

Jeremy put the plate down. "About as much as I hope this suits you, your ladyship," he said, pulling her face to his again and kissing her ardently.

"If you keep doing that, we will never get these dishes done," Meggie said. "Now behave." She put her hands in the water and resumed washing.

Jeremy pointed a finger at her. "It seems to me you are the one who was misbehaving, young lady."

"Be that as it may, we have a job to do and if you don't hurry up, I shall be finished long before you."

He gave a sharp salute. "Aye, aye, sir. Getting back to my post, sir."

The work passed quickly as they talked about the evening and the people who had come to celebrate with them. When the final dish was dried and put away, Jeremy pulled Meggie onto his knee. He leaned his head against her bosom.

"I'm so happy, Meggie - far happier than I ever thought I would be or even deserve to be. I can hardly wait ..." he hesitated. "I just wish ... we could start our lives together in the foreseeable future."

"So there is no end in sight yet?"

"No." He lifted his head and looked up at her. "But I promise you, I will not wait forever. You know I can't tell you any more, but my patience is growing thin, and if it weren't for ... the commitment I've made, I would change things immediately. Sadly, it's just not time yet."

Meggie kissed his forehead. "I'll be here, Thomas, whenever the time is right."

"Will you, Meggie? Oh, I hope so. With all my heart, I hope so. And now, I think it's time for bed. You must be tired and I know I am too."

Meggie pushed his chair to his bedroom. They kissed passionately, but their longing eyes gave way to tiredness and Meggie bade him goodnight with a last, sweet kiss.

"Sleep well, my love. I'll see you in the morning," Jeremy said, as Meggie left.

The household slept longer than usual on Christmas day, causing Nancy to bustle around the kitchen with bird-like speed when she finally came downstairs at nine o'clock.

Ian, rubbing his eyes as he sat watching her, said, "You're making me dizzy with your running around like a headless chicken. Can you not slow down a little?"

"Slow down, he says. You'd be singing a different tune if you had to wait too long for your breakfast." She continued with her food preparations until Meggie walked in.

Meggie kissed each of her parents in turn, as she wished them good morning.

"Good morning, darling. Be a dear and set the table. Your father can't seem to do anything more than sit there bothering me."

"Of course. But there's no need to race, Mum. It's Christmas morning."

"That's what I tried to tell her, but she never listens to me," Ian said.

"That's because you natter all the time," Nancy retorted.

"Good morning everyone," Jeremy said, wheeling himself into the room. "And Merry Christmas to you all."

"Merry Christmas to you, Thomas," they chorused.

Nancy McIntosh hurriedly placed platters of food on the table. "Best fill up your bellies," she said. "Ye'll be needin' your strength to walk to church."

"Thomas can't walk to church, and if he rides, he'll be breaking the law," Ian said.

Jeremy smiled. "As far as I know, there's an exception for anyone who can't actually walk. In the past, I've always taken the coach to church on Christmas Day and so far, no one's arrested me."

"If you ride, you'll need company," said Ian. "I volunteer."

"You are just a lazy old sod who doesn't want to walk," Nancy said, pointing her knife at him.

"I think it's safe for all of us to ride with Thomas. I can't imagine the Queen sending her soldiers to Tiddlebury to arrest us for breaking such a silly law. I don't know what King Edward was thinking when he passed it."

"I'm inclined to agree with you, Meggie. We'll all go together," Jeremy said.

"Riding or not, we'll have to leave soon, so eat up," Nancy said.

Chapter 23

Harrison Hall, January 1588

It was the last ball of the Christmas season and Mary intended to have as wonderful a time as she'd had in the previous weeks since her miscarriage. Conversation ceased among the older women when Mary and William entered the ballroom. She glanced around and spotted the dashing Lord Stephen Falconridge surrounded by adoring females whose eyes never wavered from his animated body and hands gesticulating gracefully to illustrate some story. Mary abruptly left William and pushed through the groups of people. She took hold of Stephen's arm and walked him away from the other women, a supercilious smile acknowledging the invisible knives they were throwing at her back.

The couple took their position on the dance floor and a ripple of nodding heads and whispers swirled around the room as Mary's flagrant behaviour again became the favourite topic of discussion. William's sour face when he turned away toward the buffet table set off another round of jokes at his expense. He wished his parents hadn't gone to the south of Italy for the winter.

Partway through the evening, Mary and Stephen contrived to absent themselves from the main hall and find a quiet alcove. Stephen took her in his arms and they kissed long and ardently.

"This is the last ball of the season," Mary said, looking up into Stephen's deep blue eyes. "What are we going to do?" she said plaintively. "Where shall we arrange to meet?"

Stephen was perplexed. He had enjoyed his trysts and dalliances with Mary for the last few weeks, but had no intention of pursuing her once the season was finished. He pulled Mary to his chest while mulling things over. The charming and beautiful Lady Martindale had not yet invited him to come to Italy with her and it might be very pleasant to have a few more assignations with Mary, an exceptionally enthusiastic bed partner. The smell of her perfumed hair delighted his senses as he whispered in her ear. "You know I want you, Mary and I have a solution. A friend of mine is away, and he won't mind if we use his home." He gave her directions to the place, a scant two hours by coach. "Next Wednesday - shall we say one o'clock? Perhaps you could arrange to stay overnight."

Mary inhaled his musky scent. "Of course I can. Oh, Stephen, I am so looking forward to that, and perhaps we can discuss our future life together?"

He smiled and cupped her face. "Let's just enjoy this evening and not worry about the future. Come now, darling, time to dance the night away."

Mary pulled him to her and kissed him passionately. She took his arm and they entered the great hall, where her gloating look caused an angry wave of jealousy to wash over the sea of watching eyes.

William's face flushed when he saw them return and his fists clenched. At least, he reminded himself, the season is over. Things will be better now.

Mary stayed in her room for the next few days under the pretext of being exhausted, taking her meals there so she would not have to come in contact with William.

Wednesday morning, she arose early and ordered the coach for eleven o'clock. William was out riding and Mary left word to say she had gone to visit a sick friend and wouldn't be back until the following day. As per her arrangement with Stephen, Mary's driver dropped her at an inn, where she told him she would catch the next coach to Exeter.

Stephen arrived shortly and greeted her with restraint for the benefit of any watching eyes. Inside the carriage, it was a different story and the ride to Folly's End was a jolly one culminating in Mary's being carried across the threshold of the imposing house.

The next twenty-four hours passed swiftly, filled with love-making, interrupted only for food and drink. Arrangements were made for Mary to come again the following week, although

Stephen would make no further commitment than that, citing his concern William might take action against one or other of them.

Only moments after returning to Harrison Hall, William came into Mary's boudoir asking where she had been. She reiterated her story of a sick friend.

"What friend?"

"What difference does it make to you? It's someone you don't know."

"You left me here all alone without company." His whiney voice grated on her ears.

"Oh, for heaven's sake, William! Your parents may be away but you were not alone. This place is full of people."

"But you're my wife and it's your company I want, Mary. Why don't you want to spend time with me? I hardly see you."

Mary sighed and rolled her eyes. "I've been off working hard to help my dear friend Elizabeth, leaving me so ghastly tired and all you can do is complain about being alone." She sat down on the bed and clutched her forehead. "You've given me a headache. I have to lie down now."

William hesitated. "Is there anything I can get for you?"

"No. Just leave me alone."

William was distressed to think he had made his wife ill, docilely turned to the door and shut it quietly on his way out.

In truth, she was tired, but not from the activities she had hinted at to William.

She did her best to avoid him for the next week, preferring to keep pleasant thoughts in her mind of what lay ahead.

Mary's tryst with Stephen was everything she had anticipated and more, as he informed her the cottage would be available to them for another week. Lady Martindale's expected invitation had not been received.

While waiting her return, William filled his day consuming vast quantities of ale which released a previously untapped anger. He staggered about their rooms, overturning anything in his way. Servants who had come running at the noise, left in fear of the wrath of the man with the blazing eyes who screamed at them.

By the time Mary returned, his extreme anger had tempered somewhat. He met her at the front door. "So you deshided to come home, did you?" he yelled as he fell against her.

Mary was appalled. "You're drunk. Get away from me!" She hurried upstairs.

William staggered after her and slammed open the boudoir door.

"I know you've been with another man. Who ish it? Shtephen?" He wove his way across the room.

"I haven't been with any man! Get out of here!"

William grabbed Mary's shoulders and breathed into her face. "You're lying!"

Mary recoiled from the fumes. "Let go of me!" She tried to shake off his arms. "You're hurting me. Let go!"

"Who was it? I can smell him on you!"

She pushed hard and he fell back onto a chair. "You cannot smell anything but your own stink which has made me sick. You're disgusting. Go away!"

"But I love you," he wailed. With great effort, he managed to get to his feet and come toward her.

Mary wanted nothing more than to get him out of her room. "I love you too, but I have a horrible headache and it's all your fault."

His anger gave way to misery, both doing battle in his foggy brain. "You love me?" He peered at her face. "Really?"

"Yes, of course. Now go away and let me lie down." She shoved him toward the door and headed for her bed.

Finally, he turned on his heel and left.

As soon as he was gone, Mary jumped off the bed and began pacing back and forth, angrily pushing her skirts behind her at each turn. She finally stopped walking, threw herself down on a chair and began furiously tapping the fingers of her right hand on the arm of the chair.

What am I going to do? I can't stand him any more. I wish he were dead!

Her fingers jolted to a stop. A whirlpool of thoughts swirled in her mind, becoming darker and darker as it descended into a cesspool of hate, evil and cunning, ending when a fatal decision was reached. It remained only to work out the details with the one person she knew who could help.

Donald.

Chapter 24

Hawkesbury Manor, February 1588

Mary hadn't seen Donald since Richard had ordered him away from Hawkesbury, but kitchen gossip made her aware of where he lived. She rode over to Hawkesbury the next day. Bobby came out when she approached the stables.

"Good afternoon, Miss," he said, grabbing the bridle.

"Bobby. Just the person I wanted to see."

His eyes opened wide in surprise. "Thank you, Miss. It's a pleasure to see you too."

"I wonder if you would do something for me," Mary said, sweetly.

"Certainly, Miss."

Mary showed him a sealed note. "I'd like you to deliver this to Donald for me. Now. It's very important."

"I will, Miss."

"It's imperative no one knows you are doing this. It must be our little secret. Do you understand?"

"Yes, Miss. I'll tell no one."

"Good lad." Mary slipped the note with some coins into his hands.

"Oh, thank you, Miss. I'll take this right away."

"Excellent. Remember ... our secret."

Mary turned her horse away and headed for the waterfall. She sat down to wait for Donald, remembering the time he had first brought her here and their adventures in the pool. She had nearly dozed off when his voice snapped her awake.

"I certainly never expected to hear from you again after you had Richard throw me out."

Mary rose to her feet . "I'm sorry about that, but it wasn't my fault. It was Catherine. She pried the information about the baby out of me and even though I swore her to secrecy, she couldn't wait to go running to Richard. I was very mad at her. You can see I'm not to blame, can't you?"   She placed her hand on his chest. Her heady perfume reminded him of times past and he had to force himself not to take her in his arms.

"What I can see is you sent a note asking me to meet you. What do you want? Is this a scheme to get me in trouble with my new employer?"

"No, of course not. I need your help."

Donald raised an eyebrow. "My help."

"Yes. We ... we have a rat problem and ... um ... I was hoping you could suggest something to get rid of them."

"Suggest something?"

"Yes, you know ... a poison or ... something."

Donald stared at her so long that she became very uncomfortable. "For rats."

"Yes."

"Or perhaps just one rat?" Donald looked at her with dark amusement. Mary turned away. He grabbed her shoulder and turned her around. "Sick of your husband already?" He pulled her roughly to him. "Doesn't please you like I did?"

"Let go of me!"

His eyes were blazing with desire and he kissed her passionately.

The familiar smell of horses and hay, coupled with his sexual heat, inflamed her senses, and her struggle to get away faded almost as fast as it had begun. Still holding each other, they sank to the ground. Donald wasted no time in raising Mary's skirts and entering her.

He rolled off and Mary lay there panting. When she caught her breath, she sat up and glared at him. "You're despicable! I came to you for help and you take advantage of me."

Donald laughed. Mary was furious and started to rise. He reached out, flipped her over her on top of him and covered her protesting mouth with his own. When his hold relaxed, Mary leaned back and looked at him. Her voice softened. "I really do need your help, Donald."

"To kill a rat."

"Yes ... er ... rats."

"So why isn't the gardener taking care of them?"

"Oh." Mary slid off Donald and straightened her skirts. "He is, but he asked me for the best method and I have no idea, of course, which is why I'm asking you."

Donald raised his eyebrows. "Not much of a gardener if he doesn't know how to take care of rodents."

"Well? What should I use?"

"To kill a ... rat, I would recommend belladonna. It works well. Did you want him to die quickly or a bit at a time?"

"Ummm, I hadn't thought about it. What would be better?"

"A bit at a time. Less suspicious that way."

"Less suspicious? " Mary's heart raced and her face flushed.

"Not that people really would wonder if rats died, would they?" Donald's mouth twisted into a cruel smile.

Mary looked away. "No, no. Certainly not."

"I can get this for you today. Perhaps you could meet me tonight."

"All right. But not too late. Where?"

"Behind your stable, if you like, say about 8 pm."

"All right. Be sure no one sees you." Mary stood.

"I shall be very careful. After all, we wouldn't want anyone to know you were going to kill a rat ... er ... rats." Donald laughed. He rose and went to Mary's horse. "Come. I'll help you up." He kissed her before cupping his hands. "Till tonight." He watched her ride away.

The stars were shining, but the moon was hiding behind a band of clouds when Mary made her way to the back of the stables. She jumped when Donald touched her shoulder. "You frightened me."

"Guilty conscience?"

"What? I have nothing to feel guilty about."

"That's good then. I have the belladonna. Now listen carefully. In this little packet are 12 berries, which taste very sweet. If you mixed them in a fruit dish and six or more were consumed by ... him, they would result in eventual death. The other is powdered root, the most deadly part of the plant. Death will occur immediately," he smiled nastily, "if you're in a hurry. Do you understand?"

"Yes."

"And be sure to wash your hands after using either of them so you don't take some by mistake." Donald placed the packets in her shaking hands.

"Th-thank you, Donald. This is very kind of you."

He pulled her close and whispered harshly in her ear. "If you ever say I gave these to you, I'll kill you. Do you understand?"

Mary gasped and drew back. "You ... you don't mean that."

"Say nothing and you'll never know." He kissed her fiercely, turned and disappeared into the darkness.

Mary's heart was racing and her hands shaking as she tucked the packets into her sleeve. She slipped up the back stairs into her quarters where she sighed a breath of relief after shutting the door. She hid the deadly packets in the bottom drawer of her cabinet.

Tomorrow it begins.

Chapter 25

Harrison Hall, March 1588

William was surprised to find Mary sitting at the breakfast table the next morning, even more surprised when she smiled and greeted him enthusiastically. He dropped on his chair.

"Don't you want to kiss me good morning?" Mary pouted slightly, tilted her head and looked at him coyly.

William stared at Mary, his mouth slightly open, confusion plain on his face. He slowly arose and came to her. She raised her chin and placed her arms around his neck. He kissed her, straightened up and stared. Mary turned back to the table.

"There. That's much better, don't you agree? You better have something to eat, William. You need to keep up your strength. Perhaps we could play a game of tennis later, if you like."

William resumed his seat, too dumbfounded to speak.

"William?"

"Uh, oh, yes. Tennis. That would be delightful, although I'm not very good at it."

What a surprise, Mary thought, but aloud said, "I'm sure you're quite wonderful, William, and I shan't be at all surprised if you beat me royally."

The opposite turned out to be true, for Mary could not bring herself to lose any game deliberately. She urged William to join her for a private dinner in their quarters that evening, and retired to her chambers to rest. Mary wrote a note to Stephen with regrets that she would be unable to see him for the next three weeks, assured him she loved him deeply and would see him again on the Wednesday of the fourth week.

Delighted at his wife's invitation, William came early to their sumptuous living area to discover a table had been set for the two of them, decorated with spring flowers and candles. Mary was dressed in an exceptionally low-cut gown and the sight of her mostly exposed bosom excited him in a manner he hadn't experienced since the early days of their marriage. Mary appeared happy and charming and William basked in this new-found glow of matrimonial harmony.

Near the end of the meal, Mary asked William to retrieve her shawl from the boudoir. As soon as he left, she added a few berries to their mixed fruit dessert. William returned and solicitously placed the shawl around her shoulders. Mary urged William to eat his fruit which he did with gusto, remarking on the delicious taste.

She proposed a toast to their future and they drank till the wine was finished. She watched him closely, and when there was no change, wondered if three berries had not been enough.

Heady with wine, William kissed his wife on her forehead, cheek, lips and the exposed mounds of her breasts. Mary had resigned herself to the realization a visit to her bed was likely, so made no resistance to William's lusty advances. She took her time undressing, William growing more excited with the removal of each garment.

Naked together in bed, William kissed Mary again and fondled her breasts. He was about to get on top of her, when he drew back.

"I don't feel so well."

"What's wrong?" Mary asked.

William got to his feet, lost his balance and fell back on the bed. "I have a terrible headache. It's too hot in here." Beads of perspiration stood out on his forehead.

"Oh my poor darling. Why don't I help you back to your bedchamber so you can lie down comfortably."

Mary helped him up, held his arm as he staggered back to his own room, where he fell on the bed. She brought a cold cloth and laid it on his forehead.

"You sleep now, William. You'll probably feel better in the morning."

"S-sorry, love."

"Shhh. Just rest."

Mary left the room, smiling.

William spent the next day in bed, Mary sitting with him, sewing. She decided to wait before using the any more berries or the powder.

A few days later, he reported the headaches were gone. Mary expressed her delight at his well-being, and slipped another tiny dose into his drink at dinner. The headaches returned, along with a condition which William said was too delicate to mention to her.

He remained in bed, and on the following day, Mary said she would like to ride over to see Catherine for a short while, provided William could manage without her. William nodded weakly.

Mrs. Pedley ushered Mary into the sitting-room where Catherine was doing needlework.

"This is an unexpected surprise. Do sit down, Mary. Mrs. Pedley, will you please bring us some tea, perhaps with a few slices of lemon cake, if Mrs. Stewart has any."

Mrs. Pedley nodded and left the room. The girls discussed pleasantries until the tea arrived. Between bites of the lemon bread, Catherine launched into a lengthy dialogue on the condition of one of their horses who seemed to be suffering from a malady which they could not diagnose. Mary interrupted at that point.

"That's a coincidence. William has some kind of ailment that's making him dizzy and causing headaches. We have no idea what it is, and he refuses to have the doctor come, saying he will get better on his own."

"Could it be something he's eaten that doesn't agree with him?"

Mary feigned surprise. "Perhaps. I hadn't thought of that, although we really haven't had anything new I can think of. I am just so very worried about him."

Catherine was at a loss to understand Mary's sudden change of attitude toward William. Remembrance of Mary's public humiliation of him at many of the events they had all attended was still strong.

"You and William must be getting along better now."

251

"Whatever are you talking about? William and I have always gotten along splendidly. He is the love of my life."

Catherine was so startled, her upper body jerked backward. "The love of your life?" she squeaked.

"Certainly. I really don't understand your surprise," Mary said, brushing an imaginary speck off her skirt. "I suppose I had better go home and see how my poor dear is feeling."

The two girls rose and walked to the door.

"It was, um, very nice of you to come by, Mary. Give William my best and tell him I hope he feels better soon."

"I will." Mary walked to her waiting coach, stopped and looked back. "Would you like to go riding tomorrow afternoon or perhaps have a game of tennis?"

It took Catherine a moment to find her voice. "I ... yes, whichever you prefer."

"Riding it is. Perhaps around one?"

"I'm looking forward to it."

Mary entered the coach and waved goodbye. Catherine stood watching it leave.

This has certainly been a day of surprises. I wonder what tomorrow will bring.

Chapter 26

Hawkesbury Manor, March 1588

The next morning, Mary expressed her delight when William said he was feeling much better. She had breakfast served in his room and stayed to eat with him. When they were finished, she asked him to come to her bedroom shortly where she had a surprise for him.

When William walked in, he found her lying on her bed in a pale pink diaphanous gown, through which could be seen her voluptuous breasts.

"Are you well enough to share my bed, do you think?" she asked seductively.

A sudden rise in the lower part of his dressing gown indicated he was at least willing. He smiled, threw off his gown and happily climbed in beside her.

He laid his hand on her cheek. "My love, you are so beautiful. I am the luckiest man in the world."

"And I, the luckiest woman."

While William fumbled through his limited ideas of lovemaking, Mary made appropriate noises and thought of her future with Stephen.

"That was wonderful. I hope you think so, Mary."

Mary snapped back to the present, suddenly aware that William was leaning on an elbow, gazing lovingly at her. "What? Oh, oh. Yes."

He smiled. "You make me so happy, Mary."

"That's nice. I'm meeting Catherine for a game of tennis this afternoon. You should rest now and I'll order lunch for you to have while I'm gone." She gave him a little push.

"But I ..."

"No arguments. I know what is best. Let me help you get your dressing gown on."

With a little more urging, William left the room and Mary drew a deep breath. She dressed, went to the kitchen, asked for a bowl of fruit for herself and ordered William's lunch to be delivered to their rooms at one o'clock. Back in her room, she removed the packets, stirred the powder into the juice of the fruit and added the rest of the berries. She placed the bowl on the lunch table and left the room to keep her date with Catherine.

Mary hummed as she went to the stables for her horse, smiled broadly when she arrived at Hawkesbury Manor and found Catherine waiting in the yard. The girls rode companionably to their favourite spot by the creek and sat down by the gurgling water.

"You're looking very happy this morning, Mary."

"It's such a nice day and William's feeling better. In fact, he made love to me this morning, so I'm very happy." She noticed Catherine's blush at the latter comment. "Why are you embarrassed about us making love. Surely you and Richard have been intimate by now."

Catherine's blush deepened. "No ... uh ... no, we haven't. We're waiting ..."

"My goodness! Waiting for what? Does Richard have a problem? Perhaps he can't ..."

"I'm sure he doesn't have a problem. We - will you keep a secret, Mary?" Her eyes danced with excitement.

"Of course. What is it?"

"Richard and I want to be married. As soon as Jeremy returns, Richard is going to ask for my hand."

"Hmmm. You don't need to be married to make love, you know."

Catherine was deflated and indignant. "Perhaps not, but that's what we want."

"He doesn't have any money. How will you be happy in a situation like that?"

"Our love isn't based on money. We will be just fine." Catherine stood and walked to the water.

"I'll keep your silly secret. There are much more juicy things to gossip about now. Did you know ..."

Catherine tuned out Mary's voice droning on about a scandal involving Lord Somebody or other. Instead, she thought of dear Richard and her heart swelled with love. She became aware Mary had stopped speaking and seemed to be waiting for an answer.

"What?"

"I said I'd better be going. I want to make sure William is still all right."

"How kind you are to him. That makes me very happy and I'm sure William is too."

"Kind to him? Of course, I am. I've always been kind to William, ever since I first met him." She walked to her horse.

Catherine rolled her eyes and followed suit.

Mary declined Catherine's offer of afternoon tea, citing William might be needing her. Catherine watched Mary ride off and went to Richard's workshop. She heard the sound of a hammer before entering and quietly opened the door, pausing momentarily to watch Richard at his work.

Aware of the sudden draft, he turned and saw Catherine. "Oh! Come in, my love, come in." He wiped the sweat off his forehead with his sleeve. "Tennis match finished already?"

Catherine leaned against the doorframe. "Yes. Mary didn't want to stay for tea. She said William isn't feeling well and might need her."

"What is wrong with William?" Richard hesitated, "And what's wrong with you, love? You don't look very happy." He came over and pulled her into a hug. "So ... what is it?"

"Nothing really." Catherine mumbled into his shoulder. "I told Mary about wanting to get married and she didn't say anything nice. In fact, she made some mean remarks."

"Oh my dear, don't worry about anything Mary says. She is just mean-spirited and I frankly don't understand how William puts up with her. Maybe she's what made him sick." Richard chuckled.

Catherine drew back and looked at him. "Now, there's a funny thing. She went on and on about how happy they are and how she has always loved William, been sweet to him and so on. And we both know she was anything but kind when she spoke of him before. I think it's very strange, don't you?"

"Perhaps we misjudged her." Richard leaned closer. "Enough of Mary." He put his hand behind her head and brought her lips to his. Catherine's response turned from tender to passionate but Richard pulled away. She looked hurt. "I want you so badly, Catherine, but I can't dishonour you and look Jeremy in the eye. You have no idea how much I wish he would return. Please understand."

Catherine nodded. "I do. And really I want the same things. If I knew how to get hold of Jeremy, I'd insist that he come home. Right now!" She stamped her foot.

Richard laughed. "That's more like it. Did you think more on going to the New World once we are married?"

"Oh yes! It will be so exciting." She grabbed Richard and twirled him around.

He leaned down and kissed her again. "You, my darling, are a delightful girl and a big distraction for me. I've got to get back to work, and I cannot do that when such a beautiful lady stands before me. Away with you and leave this poor man alone."

Catherine laughed and headed to the door singing, "Away I go, but I'll be back." The door closed. Richard smiled and returned to his work.

Chapter 27

Harrison Hall, March 1588

The closer she came to Harrison Hall, the more nervous Mary became. Thoughts of what she might find tumbled through her mind.

She began to rehearse what she would say and do when everyone found out he was dead. Of course, I will be completely innocent. William must have eaten something … could I actually say that? Cook would be blamed, but … Maybe I should have chosen another method. Shoved him out the window? He's not that heavy. I could do that, but by now, he has probably eaten the fruit. Oh dear! I must think of something else. What if Donald tells someone?

By the time she reached home, tears were beginning to fall, not for William, but for her own plight. As she climbed the stairs, her hands were shaking and her heart beating so loud she thought it would fly out of her chest.

Outside their quarters, she stood trying to calm her shaking body. Her sweaty palms slipped on the handle and with trepidation she pushed open the door.

"You're back, darling!"

Mary swooned. William rushed over to catch her. "My dear! Whatever's wrong? You are deathly pale. Come, let me help you to a chair."

Mary gasped for air as she sat down, one hand clutching the left side of her chest.

"Let me get you some wine." William rushed to the table and brought back a glass, which he held to her lips. Mary took a sip and laid her head on the back of the chair, eyes closed.

"I ... I..."

"Don't speak yet, dear. Catch your breath." William hovered over her.

Mary's shaking ceased, leaving her limp. She spoke slowly. "I don't know what came over me. It was just ... a spell of some kind. I am all right."

"You do look better; you have some colour in your cheeks."

She drew a few deep breaths and looked at the table. The fruit sat there untouched.

"Did you have tea with Catherine?"

"No. I wanted to get home to see ..."

"Oh you darling girl. You were so worried about me, you taxed yourself. I know just the thing." William walked to the table and picked up the fruit bowl and a spoon. "Some of this will make you feel better. I was just about to eat it when you came in. We can share."

"NO! I mean, no, I don't think I can eat any, William, thank you.

"Oh, do try it. How delicious it looks! See? I will have some first."

Before she could speak, William had scooped three big spoonfuls, berries and liquid, into his mouth. He swallowed quickly.

"There! It's wonderful. You will love it. Try some." William put his spoon back into the mixture. The bowl dropped from his hand and he made a gagging sound. He staggered backwards and foam started pouring from his mouth. His arms reached out, grasping the air. He fell into the table, knocking it over.

Mary jumped to her feet, her hands over her mouth, her eyes wild with a combination of fright, revulsion and terror. William was lurching around the room, his body convulsing, his eyes bulging. At last he dropped to the floor, a little foam still oozing from his mouth, the flush of his face beginning to fade. His body grew still.

Mary approached him cautiously. "William?" she whispered, but William had spoken his last and his bulging eyes stared back blankly. Mary was repulsed. She retrieved a napkin and closed his eyelids. It was time for the show to start.

Mary screamed as loudly as she could. She ran to the door and started calling for the servants. Four of them came rushing up the stairs.

"It's William. I think his heart is causing him pain. Hurry!"

The servants rushed into the room, saw the chaos and William lying on the floor. Two of the maids stopped and put their hands over their mouths. The stewards approached the body; one put his ear over William's mouth, straightened up and shook his head. The women started to cry. Soft-hearted William had been popular with the staff.

Mary shrieked and appeared about to faint. The men ran to her side and helped her to a chair. All the while, she cried, sobbed and screamed William's name.

"This cannot be. William. My poor William. His heart just stopped working. What will I do? How can I live without him?" She buried her face in her skirts.

The women came to comfort her, the men pulled a sheet from the bed to cover the body. Whispering among themselves, they decided it would be better for the grieving widow to retire to her bedchamber while the mess was cleaned up in their living quarters. The maids helped Mary out of her overskirt and into bed. She thanked them and asked she be left alone to rest.

The days following were a whirlwind of activity and arrangements for the burial service, the food to be served, letter to be written to William's parents, still holidaying in southern Italy. Mary carried out her role to perfection, saving her true thoughts and feelings for when she retired at night.   She found the continuing offers of sympathy to be the most trying and wished she could tell them the truth. No one questioned the cause of William's death, and after a couple of weeks, life returned to a more normal routine.

On the date she had promised to meet Stephen, Mary set forth with a happy heart, delighted to be out of the still sombre household. She breathed in the fresh air. With it came the realization she was free at last. She and Stephen would be married, after a suitable time of course.   Perhaps she would ignore convention and marry him sooner.

Mary was surprised to find Stephen was not waiting at the inn, but assured herself it was just like a man to forget. She rented a wagon from the innkeeper and headed for the cottage. There was a fancy coach outside the door and Mary's heart raced. Stephen was just late coming for her. On happy feet, she hurried to the door and went inside, nearly running into an assortment of luggage.

Puzzled, she went into the living-room. Sitting on the sofa was an elegantly dressed lady wearing a travel cloak and large hat. Mary stopped abruptly.

"Who are you?"

"I might ask you the same question. I am Clothilde Martindale, Countess of Manencia. And you?"

"I am ..." Mary hesitated, "looking for Stephen. We were supposed to meet here today."

Clothilde raised one eyebrow slightly and gave a small smile. "Really. How very odd. Stephen is leaving with me today to come to my villa in Italy."

Mary blanched. Her heart beat rapidly and she had trouble breathing. "Where is Stephen? I must speak to him." She went to back to the foyer. "Stephen?" she called loudly.

Stephen came from the back bedroom. His mouth fell slightly open when he saw Mary. "What are you doing here?" he asked gruffly.

"I ... we ... I wrote you I would be here today. We were ... I thought you were in love with me. William's dead. I came as soon as I could. We were supposed to be together." The words tumbled out. "You said ..."

"I said nothing at all. We had a few little get-togethers, but it was nothing serious, and I certainly never said I loved you, nor did I anticipate seeing you here today."

"But ... but ... you ... me ... we ..."

"There never was any 'we', Mary. I thought you understood that." Stephen took her by the arm and turned her toward the door. "I must ask you to leave now. As you can see, I am about to leave with the Countess, and won't be back for a long time."

Mary stopped walking and shoved his hand away. "How dare you! You know perfectly well what you told me and it certainly was NOT that you intended to run off with someone else. You led me to believe we had a future together and now it's possible because William is dead."

"I'm sorry to hear about William, but you are very mistaken in everything you said." He reached past her and opened the door. "Please leave before you embarrass yourself further."

Mary was furious. "Embarrass myself! It is you who should be embarrassed, you lecherous liar! After all I went through. I hate you!" she screamed. Her hand slapped his face. Stephen grabbed her arm and shoved her out the door, shutting it before she could regain her balance.

Mary pounded on the door. "I hate you! I hate you! I shall tell everyone what you did.   I hate you," her fists grew weaker as tears took over. She turned away and went back to the wagon. With a vicious jerk to the reins, Mary headed back to the inn.

Life was over for her here. Her hatred for Stephen overflowed onto William's unsuspecting parents, Richard and Catherine because they were happy, Donald for giving her what she had wanted, and the whole county. It was time to leave.

Chapter 28

The Crown & Anchor, May 1588

It was a night typical of those Jeremy had sat through for the last several months. The noisy laughter following the bawdy jokes, bounced off the wooden beams of the Crown and Anchor and mingled with the pungent smell of mutton stew and wood smoke. Meggie and two serving wenches jostled their way through the groping hands of murderers, thieves, scoundrels and sailors, many of whom had consumed more than their fair share of frothy ale. Each time the door opened, the mournful clang of the river's warning bell could be heard through the foggy April night air, hanging like a shroud over Tiddlebury and the

Thames.

Huddled in the back corner, eyes half-closed, Jemmy sat as usual, slouched against the wall, ignoring the noisy crowd. His mouth was now a small gap in the middle of his bushy brown beard, below his lip darkened to black by ale. Light from the candle on the small table did not improve the appearance of the scruffy shirt which covered his muscular upper torso. He remained motionless, except for the slightly twitching fingers which clutched his almost-empty mug.

Two men sat quietly at a nearby table, exchanging only a few desultory remarks about the rest of the patrons. To the casual observer, they appeared to be merely gazing at the crowd. Someone watching more closely would have noticed their periodic, surreptitious glances at the door, barely visible through the sea of bodies. Parker's scarred face,

crooked nose and ruddy complexion made him indistinguishable from the rest of the riff-raff. Brooks, taller and thinner, had disguised his finer features with smudges of dirt, and guaranteed his anonymity by wearing a nondescript dark jerkin and cap.

Meggie approached Jeremy and smiled shyly. "How are you doing, luv? Need a refill?" she asked kindly.

Unmoving, the man replied softly, "No th-thanks, Meggie. Ah've enough f-f-fer now."

Outwardly, Meggie's expression did not change, but she smiled to herself at his common speech. "Righty-o then, Thomas. You just call if you want something" Turning to the other two men, Meggie continued, "And what about you two gents. Can I get you anything?"

Parker leered at Meggie's flushed face and bouncing bosom. "Lift yer skirts and I'll take whatcher got there," he said, making a grab for her waist with his meaty hand.

Used to the rough men who came daily to the waterfront tavern, Meggie adroitly moved aside, tossed her head and flounced off, ignoring the laughter that followed her.

"You better leave these wenches alone tonight, Parker. Keep your mind on the business at hand."

"I'd keep me mind on me business if 'e's lordship'd git here," Parker replied, looking once again at the door. "Can't see naught from 'ere anyways." He moved his head sideways trying to see the door. "Hold on. I thinks that's 'im."

Brooks followed Parker's glance. A tall, slender man with jet black hair and trim mustache was making his way through the crowd. Despite his workman's clothes, his arrogant bearing and disdainful countenance marked him as someone who did not normally patronize this type of establishment.

"Drunken protestant pigs," he said with a heavy Spanish accent, as he took the vacant chair opposite Parker.

"Keep your voice down, Esteban. We wouldn't want that accent of yours giving away the show," replied Brooks.

Riotous screams of laughter erupted from the middle of the room as a barmaid was hoisted onto the table top.

"Dansh for us, Bess." The coarse, besotted voices continued. "Go on. Show us whatcher can do."

"I'll show you what she can do." To the delight of the exuberant crowd, a burly man lifted her off the table and threw her into their waiting arms, eliciting more shouts and laughter.

"Madre de Dios! Look at them! They are too drunk and stupid to see anything going on under their noses."

"Forget them. What word do you bring us from Spain?" inquired Brooks.

"Is it safe to talk here?" Esteban Vasquez asked in Spanish, as he around. His dark, cautious eyes came to rest on Jeremy Hawkins nodding in the corner. "What about him?"

"Yer means that crippled lump?" Parker looked at Jeremy and snorted. "Yer don't 'aveter worry about 'im. 'Is mind don't work too good and 'e kin barely speak the Queen's English let alone Spanish. Me Spanish ain't too good neither, so yer might 'ave ter talk a bit of English as well."

Vasquez raised an eyebrow at the irony, then looked at Brooks for confirmation. Brooks nodded his head. "It's safe."

Meggie appeared once more at their table. "Does the gentleman want a drink?" she said, eyeing Vasquez.

Afraid of an outburst of contempt from Vasquez, Brooks hastily replied, "None of us wants anything right now."

Parker grinned and winked. "Maybe later, darlin', if yer lucky I'll meetcher out back."

"I'd have to be stone blind and dead drunk afore I'd let the likes of you lay a hand on me." Meggie turned away swiftly to escape the expected slap on the buttocks.

After she was out of earshot, Vasquez glanced around. Noting Jeremy's head was now lolling on his chest and no one else was paying any attention to them, he began speaking. "Now to business. First tell me what is happening in the Court. Any whispers? Rumours?"

"Not about Spain. Her Majesty's too busy trying to appease those who are still upset with her for ordering Mary's execution last year," responded Brooks.

"Aye, that and trying to figure where she'll send that scoundrel, Drake, next. It's been two years since Santo Domingo and she's always lookin' fer more booty," added Parker.

Vasquez leaned closer to the other men. "Good. They must be kept in the dark. At our end, the time is set. With the blessing of Pope Sixtus, the Duke of Medina Sedonia will sail from Portugal on May 30th. He has outfitted 125 vessels - an invincible Armada," Vasquez said proudly.

"So the Armada should arrive in the Channel somewhere in mid-July," said Brooks. "What then?"

"The Armada will link up with the Duke of Parma in the Spanish Netherlands at Calais, and will ferry the Duke's soldiers across the Strait of Dover. From there, they'll march on London and seize the Queen. Then England will come under the rightful rule of King Phillip as designated by Mary, and, in accordance with God's wishes, the true church will prevail. It will be my personal pleasure to see El Drague beheaded for his infamous acts against my country. After that, Spain will become the unquestionable ruler of the seas, and those who have supported us will see their fortunes increase beyond their wildest dreams," Vasquez finished confidently.

"What would you like us to do?" asked Brooks.

"You must pass the word amongst the Catholic rebels. Tell them to gather their weaponry and have their Spanish flags ready to fly. Their homes must be recognizable to the soldiers when they arrive."

Parker leaned across the table. "What about me boys? They's good fighters and they's been lookin' forrard ter see some action," he said. "'ow's about they marches with them soldiers what's comin' across?"

Vasquez leaned away to escape Parker's foul breath and thought for a moment. "Do they have weapons?"

"Aye. And them what don't 'ave proper ones will bring clubs and shovels."

"Very well then. They can join the soldiers on the march to London. Make sure your men are wearing red armbands with a black 'S' sewn in. This is how they will be identified as members of the true faith. Can you arrange for food and drink to be on hand for the soldiers?"

"I'll get word to me boys tomorrow. Of course, a lot of them ain't got much to spare - not like 'is nibs' friends," Parker said slyly, nodding at Brooks.

Vasquez stared hard at Parker. "This may help," he said, pushing a bag of coins across the table. "Spend it wisely," he warned, an unmistakable threat in his tone.

"Yer can count on me, guv," Parker said, smiling as he quickly grabbed the leather pouch, hefted its weight and happily stuffed it inside his waistband.

"You will report to Brooks here when you have made all the arrangements, understood?"

" 'appy to do that. We'll be right ready." Parker smiled from ear to ear.

Turning to Brooks, Vasquez continued, "The soldiers will need temporary quarters in London before returning to Spain and The Netherlands. Can you provide this?"

"I had thought as much," Brooks responded, " and have the names of families where all the men will be welcome." Reaching in his pocket, he passed a folded paper to Vasquez. "These people have been stockpiling food since our last meeting."

"Excellent. It seems everything is set. Do you have any questions?"

Both men shook their heads.

"Good. You have done well and you shall be handsomely rewarded for your efforts." Vasquez gave a satisfied smile. "Now I can thankfully take my leave of this abominable place. I shall not see you again until Phillip sits on the throne of England. Vaya con Dios." He rose and pushed his way through the throng of revelers.

Parker watched Vasquez until he was lost from view. "Can't say I'll be sorry not ter have ter see 'im again. 'Is eyes gives me the shivers. Wouldn't want ter be on the wrong side of 'im. I'll bet 'e's got one of them thin blades shoved up 'is sleeve."

"You'll want to see him quick enough for your gold, I'll bet."

"Aye, that's true. But yer can count on me takin' me own friends with me when I does."

"It's time to get out of here," Brooks said, rising. "I've got things to do and so do you. Send me a messenger when you have your arrangements completed. Let's go."

"I'm thinkin' I just might stay a bit, maybe find a wench or two fer the night," said Parker.

"Not tonight, my friend. You'd best get out of here before the gold in that pouch disappears. Come along," Brooks replied, taking his arm.

"All right, then. Stiff-necked uppity crust. A man needs ter relax a bit yer know," grumbled Parker, reluctantly allowing himself to be pushed toward the door.

A pair of dark blue eyes watched their progress. Once they were out of sight, Jeremy raised his mug to catch Meggie's attention.

When she finally looked over, he pointed toward the door. Meggie nodded and spoke to Ian who was busy behind the bar. He immediately left his position, and opened the door at the back of the room.

Approaching Hawkins' table, he inquired kindly, "Ready to go to bed, are you, Thomas?"

"Yes please, Ian. But I also want to let you know I must leave before daylight tomorrow."

Ian was taken aback. "As sudden as this?"

"I'm sorry it's like that, Ian, but something has happened that requires me to go home as quickly as possible."

"I hope there's naught wrong with your family," Ian's voice was full of concern.

"No, no. Nothing like that."

"Can't be helped then. Sorry I am to see you go, laddie. Will you be coming back to see us again?"

"You can count on that, Ian. I will come back. I'm just not sure when, but it's time for me to go now. Could I trouble you to make sure I get up early in the morning?"

"It'll be no trouble at all. Are you ready to go to your room now?"

"Yes, if you have a minute."

Ian pushed the table aside and wrapping Jeremy's arm around his neck, hoisted him with ease over his shoulder. Stepping through the open door, Ian remarked as he always did, "Watch your head, laddie."

As they approached Jeremy's room, Ian remarked, "Good job the wife's got a candle burning for us." He continued on to the kitchen and called to Nancy. "Mrs. McIntosh, bring us a lantern, will you? Thomas is going to his room now."

"I'm coming, Ian." Following these words, the matronly figure of Nancy McIntosh came bustling down the hall. "It's early tonight you are, Thomas, and a good thing too. You're too fine a gentleman to be mixing with the likes of them ruffians who came in tonight. Of course, I've told you that before."

"You don't need to worry any more, Nancy. He's off home in the morning," Ian said.

Nancy looked shocked. "Oh! Sorry I am to hear that, Thomas. You've finished your book then?"

"I have indeed."

Nancy paused for breath as she opened the bedroom door, then began again. "Watch how you put him down, Mr. McIntosh. Not on the bed, ye daft man. He'll have to clean up some afore retiring."

"Whist woman, stop your natterin'. I've been bringing him in here for months. Do ye really think I don't know what I'm doing?"

Jeremy laughed at their exchange, then grunted as Ian placed him into his wheeled chair next to the table.

"Ye only know what to do because I tell you." Nancy's gray curls, peeking from under her cap, bobbed with authority. "Now away with you man and tend to yon thieves who like as not are sneakin' out the door while you're lollygagging about in here."

"Ian, would you mind sending Adam to me?"

"Aye, I'll do that," Ian said, as he closed the door behind him.

"I'll just throw another log on the fire. The night's chill goes right through a body's bones." Nancy turned back from the fire. "Thomas, if you're all right, I'll go make you a nice cup of tea."

"That would be lovely, Nancy. You are too kind. If it wasn't for these useless legs, I'd dance you around the room."

"Away with you, wasting your charms on an old woman like me." Nancy blushed, chuckled to herself and left the room amid a swirl of petticoats.

Once alone, Jeremy pulled the writing materials to him and hastily scribbled all he had overheard Vasquez tell Parker and Brooks. A knock sounded on the door.

"Come in."

"You sent for me, Master Thomas?" Cap in hand, Adam stood deferentially at the door.

"Yes. Come right in and close the door, Adam."

"Aye, sir."

"I have an errand for you to run. You must do it tonight and quickly. Is it still foggy out?"

"Aye. She's a regular pea souper all right. Do I 'ave to go far, sir?" A worried look crossed Adam's young face.

"To Captain Hawkins' house. You know where that is."

"Aye, sir. But it's awful dark." He lowered his voice. "A good night for a murder." Adam's brown eyes widened in fright as he contemplated what might be his fate.

"Can't very well murder you if they can't see you, right Adam?" Jeremy smiled reassuringly.

"Oh. That's right, sir. Never thought of that, sir. Guess it'll be all right then." Confidence restored, Adam brightened, squared his shoulders and grinned. "You can count on me, sir."

"I know I can, Adam. Now you must take a horse, go to Captain Hawkins' house and ask for Anthony Turner. Hand this directly to Anthony Turner personally, do you understand? Do not give it to anyone else. And you must tell no one what you are doing. This is an extremely important message. Your future and everybody else's depends on your delivering this to him." Jeremy handed Adam a folded paper. "Put this somewhere safe on your person where it won't get lost - perhaps in your boot."

"That's a good idea, sir." Adam tucked the paper carefully inside. "She be safe in there for sure."

"After you have seen Mr. Turner, I want you to come back here and tell me. There will be a reward waiting for you."

"Oh thank you, sir. I'll be right quick, I will."

"Good lad. Godspeed. The fate of England rests in your hands."

"Aye sir!" Full of importance and eager to complete his mission, Adam darted from the room, nearly colliding with Nancy and her tea tray.

"Mercy! Watch where you're going, you little urchin."

"Sorry, missus," Adam called, disappearing down the hall.

"Never saw him in such a hurry afore. You must have put a flea in his ear. I've brought you a nice cup of tea and a fresh scone Thomas."

"It looks wonderful, Nancy. I wonder if I might ask another favour of you?"

"Of course you can. Ask away."

"Could you bring me a bowl of hot water? You will be happy to know that I am at last going to remove this ghastly beard, or most of it anyway."

"Thankful I am to hear that. You look like a wild man peeking out from behind those bushes. It'll take a while to get heated, but I'll be right back when it's ready. You drink up your tea now."

Time passed swiftly as Jeremy thought about his future while finishing his snack. His reverie was interrupted by a rapid knock on the door. "Mr. Thomas sir, it's me, Adam."

"Come in."

"I've delivered your note sir, right to Mr. Turner like yer told me."

"Good, good. Did he give you a message for me?"

"Yes. He said tell Master Thomas he'd be off immediately and for him - that means you - to be bloody careful. Oh, excuse me, sir, that's my word - bloody. But he did say be careful and godspeed."

"You've done well, Adam. Here's your reward as promised."

Adam eagerly took the coins. "Thankee, Master Thomas, thankee."

"Run along now, it's getting late."

"Yes sir, thankee, sir. Good-night, sir." Adam hurried to the door and raced out, almost colliding with Nancy for the second time.

"Whist, laddie! Do you ever walk anywhere? Always running, never looking where you're going."

"Sorry, missus. G'night, missus."

Nancy placed a steaming bowl of water in front of Jeremy. "I've brought you my best reflector," she said proudly, propping a shiny square of tin in front of him. Smiling, she added, "You can see how awful you look now."

Jeremy regarded his reflection. "You're right, Nancy. That's a face that would scare the devil himself." Under Nancy's watchful eye, Jeremy carefully trimmed back the scraggly beard he had allowed to grow at will for more than a year.

"Oh my. I can't believe it! You look like a different man!"

Jeremy smiled. "That's the general idea, Nancy. Does this meet with your approval?"

Nancy gazed at the curving mouth and twinkling eyes of the handsome twenty-six year old. "Och aye, and I'm sure Meggie ... er ... the lassies will love it too. Now I'll just clean up all this mess so you can get some sleep." Nancy tossed the wash water out the window and gathered up the dishes. "Will you be all right now, Thomas? Is there anything else you need?"

"No, that's everything thank you, except I want to wish you farewell," Jeremy said, taking her hand. "As you know, my time here is over, Nancy. I'll be leaving before daybreak tomorrow, but I want you to know that I'll never forget you and Thomas and all your kindness to me." He kissed her work-worn hand.

Nancy retrieved a handkerchief from her pocket and surreptitiously dabbed at her brown eyes. "So it's to be tomorrow, is it?" She sniffled.

"Come now, don't be sad. You should be happy to get rid of a miserable burden like me. Besides, you have my promise that some day I'll see you again. I think you know I am leaving my heart behind me and must come back to claim it. And perhaps someday you will visit me at my home."

"We don't even know where that is. Besides, Ian would never leave the tavern."

"Get rid of Ian then, and I'll marry you myself. Then we can live happily together forever and ever."

"Oh, you're an awful man. What nonsense you talk! I'm old enough to be your mother." Nancy blushed, her words belying her pleasure. "Besides, I think our Meggie would have something to say about that, so you best see you do come back. You'll always be welcome here." Her spirits restored, Nancy picked up the bowl and lantern and went to the door.

"I promise. Good-night, Nancy."

"Good-night, Thomas. Godspeed on the morrow." Nancy closed the door softly behind her.

Jeremy sighed. He would miss these good people while he was gone and hoped his ability to return would come sooner rather than later. He swiftly packed his bags then used his powerful arm muscles to hoist himself into bed.

Although his body was tired, Jeremy's mind was wide awake. Watching the fire cast wavering shadows on the wall, he lay for a while thinking of his seafaring brother, John, who would no doubt head to London once he heard from his valet, Turner. He would be aiding their cousin, Francis Drake, now Vice-Admiral of the English Navy, and Lord Howard prepare the English fleet for the coming of the Spanish Armada. After all these months, it seemed rather anti-climactic the end had come so quickly.

Sounds drifted to his room of the revelers calling to one another as they left the inn, and in his mind's eye, he saw Meggie and Ian closing up for the night. His heart ached at the thought of leaving Meggie behind, although he realized he had no other option. Until such time as he was sure that his life was in no danger, it was far safer to leave her here in the care of her parents.

Certain he was Meggie would appear, especially after she learned he would be leaving in the morning, and it was not too long after hearing the customers leave, a light knock came on his door.

Meggie stepped quietly into the room. "Are you awake, Thomas?"

He saw her distraught face. "Come here, my love." He held out his arms. She started toward him but stopped, her eyes opening wide. "Who is this in Thomas's bed?"

Jeremy laughed. "An improvement, do you think?"

"An improvement beyond anything I would have thought possible. You look so different."

"Do you like the look of this different someone?"

"I knew you were a good-looking man, but I had no idea of how truly handsome you are."

"Stop complimenting me and come here. I want to hold you in my arms tonight of all nights."

Meggie threw herself on the bed beside Jeremy and buried her face in his shoulder. Her voice was muffled as she said, "It's true then. You're leaving in the morning?"

"I am. My time here is finally finished."

She turned her head and sobbed against his chest.

"There, there, love. Don't cry. I know it's hard to say goodbye, but look at it as the beginning of our future together. At long last, we can actually think about that. First, I must go home and wait to make sure it is safe for me to be with you, and then I will return."

"Why wouldn't it be safe for you to be here?"

"Because something has happened, and you know I can't talk about that."

Meggie drew her hand softly against the scar on his jaw-line. "Does this have something to do with why you can't tell me anything?"

Jeremy smiled. "No, that scar is the result of being charged by a bull when I was much younger."

"A bull! It is a wonder that is the only reminder you have."

"Not the only one." He tapped his legs. "These too."

"I am so sorry, Thomas. You must have suffered greatly."

"It's long ago in the past, Meggie, and I have you to think about now and our life together. You must trust me we belong together and nothing is going to prevent that. We are soul mates, meant to be together, as I'm sure we have in previous lives. I love you so much, Meggie, and there will never be anyone else in this world for me. You do believe me?"

"I do. And I feel the same, Thomas ... er, are you free now to tell me who you are?"

Jeremy drew in a deep breath. "No, I best not, Meggie. Please just trust me you will not be disappointed by my background once you learn the truth, which will be when I come back to claim you as my bride."

"Oh, Thomas, I do want that so much. Have you any idea how long that will be?"

"Unfortunately, no. But it will be the very minute I know I can. Please believe me."

"I do. And you know I will wait for you a lifetime, if that's what it takes."

Jeremy chuckled. "Hopefully, it won't be that long, Meggie. God would not punish us like that." He pulled her face to his and kissed her lightly. "I cannot possibly wait a lifetime."

Their lovemaking that night had the added element of sweet sorrow, encompassing a passion of two lovers who were uncertain if they would ever be together again. Neither wanted to let the other go, but an uneasy sleep finally overtook them.

At a touch on his shoulder, Jeremy awoke with a start. Momentarily disoriented, he couldn't understand why Ian was standing over him holding a lantern. "You've slept a bit over, laddie. It's time you were on your way."

Memory returned and Jeremy looked guiltily around, then thankfully realized Meggie was gone. Breathing deeply, he hoisted himself up. "Thank you for waking me, Ian. I'll just be a minute."

"Nancy's sent you a cup of tea. You'd best be drinking it, else I'll be getting a talking to."

Jeremy dressed hurriedly and consumed his beverage. Once more Ian hoisted him around his shoulders and, with Jeremy carrying the lantern, made the trip out the back door.

"I'll go fetch your wheeled chair," Ian said.

Jeremy turned up the collar of his cloak and pulled his hat down low to help cover up his nearly beardless face.

Ian returned with the chair. "Now, where is that confounded lad? I told him to be here with the horse and cart."

An animal snorted to his left. "Ah, there you be." Ian could barely see the outline of the horse waiting in the shadows.

"Good girl. Hold steady. Adam, where are you?" Not receiving any response, Ian hoisted the chair into the cart and lifted Jeremy up as well. Jeremy adjusted his hooded cloak to conceal his face from any watchers.

"Good thing that horse snorted. Can't see a blasted thing in this blackness. Adam," Ian called again. "Where is that jackanapes? I'll skin him alive."

"Here, I'm right here, Mr. McIntosh. Sorry, Mr. Thomas. I just had to ..."

"Spare us the details, lad. You're supposed to be mindin' this here horse. What if it had wandered off? How'd Mr. Smithson be getting home then?"

"Never mind, Ian. It's all right. He's here now. Again thanks for all your help, my friend."

"Twas a pleasure havin' ye, laddie. God bless you on your journey. Be careful. There might still be bad ones hanging about down here," Ian said worriedly. "And Adam, you see to it that you get back here quickly after you see Mr. Smithson on his way. You've got chores to do."

"Yer can count on me, Mr. McIntosh," Adam replied.

"We'll be fine, Ian. Farewell, my friend, until we meet again."

The darkness swallowed up the cart before Ian closed the door. Jeremy glanced back with sorrow in his heart, as he wondered when he would come this way again.

Adam wound his way through the streets leading away from the docks and up the hill to the outskirts of town. He bid Jeremy farewell and scurried back through the streets he knew so well. Jeremy watched him go, then turned north to the home he had left so long ago.

Chapter 29

Home to Hawkesbury, Late May 1588

Further from the river, the fog lessened and the road became visible in the dim light of approaching dawn. Taking the less beaten tracks extended his travel time to a fortnight, and Jeremy was exhausted by the time he reached Hawkesbury.

Driving up the lane in mid-morning sunshine, he was overcome with relief and weariness. The wing on either side of the main house seemed to be reaching to welcome him home. He turned his head at the sound of pounding of hoof-beats rapidly growing louder on his right. Approaching at great speed was a magnificent chestnut mare ridden by a young woman whose streaming hair, ignited by the sun, appeared as flames chasing the duo. When Catherine at last noticed him, she slowed her horse, circled behind the cart and came up alongside Jeremy.

"My God, Jeremy! Is that really you? How wonderful to see you! Why didn't you warn us? Shame on you for not getting word to us. We would have made preparations for a proper homecoming. Where have you been? What have you been doing? Does anyone else know you're here or will I be the first to spread the alarm?" To the prancing horse, she continued, "Easy, girl."

"Catherine, my darling sister. Still at a loss for words, I see." Jeremy laughed as he gazed at her rosy cheeks and bright blue eyes. "And untamed as ever. I thought we agreed before I left there would be no more racing ..."

"Oh, pooh! Not even in the door yet and already starting the big brother lecture. Besides, it wasn't my idea. Lightning decided she wanted to run and I just couldn't stop her. Furthermore, if you are going to scold me, Jeremy Hawkins, you can just turn that cart right around and leave again. You always make me feel like a child, when I'm really a grown woman of eighteen. I'm positively ancient!" Leaning toward Jeremy, she continued, "Also, you are not allowed to tease me because I am a lady now for certain." With a bob of her head, Catherine poked her tongue out for emphasis.

Jeremy's laughter filled the air. "The act of a lady indeed! Off you go and get Richard to help me get my chair down from the cart. And get that poor horse taken care of," he called to her departing back.

His spirits considerably lifted and still smiling, Jeremy watched his sister disappear around the back of the stately home.

As the cart came to a stop in the circular drive, the double front doors opened wide and Richard came hurrying through.

"Master Jeremy! How wonderful to have you home," he said, running down the steps.

"Richard, my friend! I'm glad to be here. And what's with the 'Master' business?"

"Mother's watching," hissed Richard, as he placed the wheeled chair on the ground.

Glancing up, John saw a frowning Evelyn Pedley standing in the doorway. He raised his eyebrows and glanced sympathetically at Richard. "I see nothing's changed."

"Oh, there've been some changes, Jemmy, but we'll talk about that later. Let's get you down," Richard said, reaching up to pull Jeremy from the cart.

"Nice to see you, Mrs. Pedley," said Jeremy, as Richard placed him in his special chair and wheeled him inside.

"Thank you, Master Jeremy," she replied stiffly, closing the doors. "Your quarters are clean and ready for use even though you did not see fit to advise us of your return. We have kept them that way since your departure last year."   Mrs. Pedley retreated to the kitchen, while Richard continued pushing Jeremy toward the west wing of the house.

"You will have to tell us of all your travels, Jeremy. I can't wait to hear what your school was like."

"I'm afraid you are going to be vastly disappointed, Richard. I really didn't do much at all. It's pretty quiet in here. Where are Mary and Aunt Annabelle?"

"They aren't here any longer, Jemmy."

"Why not? They were supposed to stay until I got back."

"That's a bit of a long story and just some of what we have to tell you. You look very tired. Perhaps it would be a good idea to wait till after you're rested before bringing you up-to-date."

"You're right. I am rather tired. Whatever's happened is over."

Entering his own sitting-room, Jeremy looked around and smiled, pleased to be home in his own surroundings. "My news can wait also. Why not ask Catherine to get a picnic lunch ready and if you wake me in a couple of hours, we three can escape old owl-face and catch up on everything. We can always sit in the summerhouse if the wind isn't too chilly. Sound all right to you?"

"Perfect. Just like the old days. Can I do anything else for you?"

"Not right now, but when you come to wake me, please bring some wash water with you."

"I will certainly do that. Is that all?"

"Yes, thanks."

Jeremy sank back on the comfortable bed, drew up the covers and was soon fast asleep. What seemed like less than a minute later, he was awakened by a cheerful voice.

"So you are alive, old sleepyhead. And about time, too. It's a beautiful day and we're starving."

Slowly opening his eyes, Jeremy found himself staring into Catherine's animated face. He groaned. "But I just got to sleep."

"Phooey! You went to sleep two hours ago and we have a marvelous lunch ready to take on our picnic. Isn't that right, Richard," she said, looking over her shoulder. "I hope you are well-rested because we want you to tell us absolutely everything. I want to know all about your adventures. I hope you met many interesting people and saw wondrous things."

"Catherine, if you don't stop talking and get out of here so I can get dressed, we are never going to make it to the pond in time for lunch. Now get!"

"Oh, as if I've never seen your undergarments before! But I'll leave. I just don't want you blaming me for dying of starvation. Of course, you will anyway. You always do."

"Catherine!"

"I'm going. Richard, make sure Jeremy hurries up." Tipping her head back, Catherine placed one hand on her forehead and the other on her stomach, and with mournful eyes and droopy mouth, continued, "I'm so famished, I just might faint."

The two young men burst into laughter as Catherine quickly disappeared out the door.

"She has lost none of her ability to delight and charm, I see," Jeremy said, still smiling.

"Indeed not. She is the brightest sun that shines around here. She brings joy into my life ... uh, everyone's life that is."

A quizzical look passed over Jeremy's face, but he mentally shook his head and finished dressing.

"Let's go out this way, Richard," Jeremy said, indicating the garden windows. "We'll beat Catherine to the pathway."

Richard quickly pushed Jeremy outside, past the awakening gardens and onto the path leading to the summerhouse and the pond at the back of the property.

Atop one of the stones guarding the bridge sat Catherine, with a satisfied look on her face. "You'll have to get up earlier than that to beat me, Jeremy Hawkins. Come and help me down, Richard, please."

Richard obliged and, with skipping steps, Catherine proudly led the way over the bridge and into the summerhouse where she had set the table with the provisions from the kitchen. All three of them were ravenous and the meal was soon demolished.

"Now you must tell us everything that happened, Jeremy. And please don't tell me you spent your entire time with your head stuck in your stuffy old books. Tell me about the parties and balls and what you did."

Jeremy had rehearsed his story often on the way home. "My dear Catherine, you are right, of course. I couldn't study all the time. it was wonderful. The Dean of the university took a shine to me and included me on the guest list for the many functions that went on. The ladies still wear stiff, pleated ruffs even bigger than before, that stand out from the tops of their dresses, which are cut daringly low. The talk is the Queen has ordered all her ball gowns to be cut extremely low so that no one will notice her face, which they say is quite homely. The gentlemen are elegant also, strutting like peacocks with their embroidered breeches and long stockings. They all have lacy handkerchiefs and affect snooty airs that would never suit you, so don't waste your time pining after one of those aristocratic fops."

"I am not 'pining' after anything, certainly not men who look like peacocks. Mary's the one who would want to know all that stuff. I just want to know if you did anything exciting, like fighting Scottish dragons or something."

Jeremy laughed. "Scottish dragons indeed! Where do you get your ideas? And speaking of Mary, why isn't she here? And Aunt Annabelle."

Richard and Catherine looked at each other.

"It's ...um... rather delicate," Richard said, looking at Catherine.

"Phooey. I'm the one she told, after all and I know more about what happened."

"Told what? Is one of you going to tell me or do I have to shake it out of you?" Jeremy said.

"I'll tell you," Catherine said. "It's really a secret and no one knows the first part except Richard, me and Mrs. Stewart, sort of, so you must never tell anyone else."

"Mary found herself in an, uh, unfortunate condition," Richard said.

"Unfortunate for everybody else maybe. But she brought it on herself, and you know it, Richard."

"I'm not sure I'm understanding this. Perhaps you should leave, Catherine, and let Richard tell me."

"Nonsense! Richard will beat around the bush. I'll tell you what happened. We found this out in bits and pieces, but here's the final story. You remember poor, sweet Mary, the cousin you thought would be a good idea to keep me company while you were gone? According to her, Donald - you remember our stable boss - took advantage of her one day when she was feeling homesick. Fiddlesticks in my opinion. Donald claimed that Mary threw herself at him - and that seems far more likely, as I saw the way she behaved around him."

"Donald? Donald did this?"

"I took the liberty of firing Donald," Richard said, "and hiring another man from St. John-on-the-Hill. I hope you don't mind."

"Certainly not, Richard. You were left in charge, and I would have done the same thing." Jemmy shook his head slightly. "My mind is reeling."

"And a good thing too. I never did trust the way Donald looked at Mary. Even so, I still don't think Mary told the right way of it."

"Perhaps it would be easier to follow if you could just tell me without your opinions thrown in, Cathy."

"Hmpf! Well ... Mary became pregnant and found herself in a quandary because she didn't want to marry Donald - not that he wanted anything to do with her. That's what he said, not my opinion," Catherine said pointedly. "She concocted a scheme to convince William Harrison to marry her and then told him she was pregnant as a result of their first ... um ... getting married. Imagine! After spurning him from the first day they met, she told him she was in love with him! Mary was just lucky William was silly enough to believe her. He was mad about her and happily jumped at the chance to get married."

"Mary and William are married?" Jeremy said.

"Married at the beginning of October last year, but ..." Richard said.

"Don't jump ahead of my story please Richard," Catherine said smiling. "The irony is Mary had a miscarriage in December - right here - so she needn't have married anyone."

"So now she's living at Harrison Hall," Jeremy said.

"You men are so impatient. I haven't finished yet."

Jeremy sighed. "Pardon me. Go ahead."

"She cried all through the wedding, which I thought was silly, the crying I mean, not the wedding - oh, I just remembered - afterwards she went back home to recuperate, although she claimed her nerves would never be the same."

"Recuperate from the wedding?"

"No, silly. From the miscarriage. But that's not all."

Jeremy groaned. "There's more?"

"Aunt Annabelle went home after the wedding, and even though Mary said she was still delicate from the miscarriage, she attended every ball of the winter season. It was quite a scandal."

"What was?"

"Mary's behaviour. She latched onto Lord Stephen Falconridge like a leech - left poor William standing by himself at all the balls. Everybody remarked on it and made fun of William for being so blatantly cuckolded. We all noticed Mary and Stephen would disappear for a while during the evening, and people were speculating on what they were doing."

"Good heavens!" Jeremy said, being drawn into the story.

"After the season was over, the most amazing thing happened. Mary came over here one day, quite unexpectedly, for a visit. She told me William had been sick and that she was quite worried about him. It surprised me she would be worried at all, and she went on to say she had always loved William and treated him kindly. I tell you, Jeremy, I was speechless."

"Now THAT is really news." Jeremy laughed and Richard joined in.

"Hush, you two. She invited herself over here the next day to play tennis with me. Of course, I said 'yes', as you are always telling me to improve my manners. She came for tennis but went right home after the match, saying she was still concerned about William. She also indelicately mentioned they had made love that morning." Catherine blushed. "I'm a little mixed up as to timing because it has been a while, but we received word that William had died. To say we were shocked would be an understatement."

"How awful! What happened? Did he have an accident?"

"No. It seems it was his heart. It just stopped working. I thought it rather strange, but that was the word Harrison Hall officially related. A short time after that, Mary returned to her former home, where she is living still with her parents, as far as we know."

"My goodness. There certainly was a lot of excitement while I was gone."

Richard nodded his head. "Indeed it was a lot of commotion."

"I should say, but as you have taken care of the details, it looks like we're back to normal," said Jeremy. He noticed Catherine and Richard exchange looks.

"What? Is there more?"

"I think I'll leave you two gentlemen and go for a walk."

Jeremy was astounded. "I've never known you to leave a conversation willingly, Catherine. Are you ill?"

"No, silly. I just feel like walking and Richard probably wants to talk to you, so ... I'll leave."

Looking very puzzled, Jeremy folded his arms. "I don't think I'll ever understand women. What about you, Richard?"

"I don't profess to understand all women. The fact is, I really don't know too many. But I know why Catherine left. She wants me to talk to you about something, or perhaps I should say, she knows I want to talk to you."

Richard stood, shoved his hands in his pockets and walked to the edge of the summerhouse. With his back to Jeremy, he said, "I don't know exactly how to begin."

"What is it? You've got me really worried now. Is there a problem with the estate? Is Catherine ill?"

"Oh no, nothing like that."

"Is it your health? Your mother? Come on, Richard, we've been friends for years. There isn't anything you can't tell me."

Richard turned and faced his companion. "Catherine and I are in love with each other."

Jemmy's face darkened. "Have you dishonoured my sister, Richard?"

Richard flushed. "Certainly not! I would never do anything to bring disgrace on Catherine or you. But we do love each other, and I want to marry her, Jeremy."

"What?! Nonsense, Richard! She's only a child."

"A child is the last thing she is, Jeremy. She will be nineteen in October and has grown up while you were gone. Catherine has spirit and determination, a will of her own, and a marvelous sense of adventure. I love her, Jeremy, and I would like your permission to marry her."

Jeremy expelled a deep breath and sat contemplating the sunlight now dappling the table. Several moments passed as he thought of the crisis ahead, his possible future and that of his sister's, and lastly of the character of the man who stood before him. He knew Richard was honest, trustworthy and with his muscular, solid build, fully capable of protecting Catherine if necessary. Finally, he looked at Richard's earnest gray eyes. "Does Catherine want this too?"

"Yes, yes, oh yes, I do." Catherine popped from around the door of the summerhouse and ran to Richard's side. "Oh please say yes, Jeremy, please. You must. Please."

"How can I refuse such a plea? Yes, you may marry, if that's what will make you happy, Catherine."

Catherine threw her arms around Jeremy, hugging and kissing him all over his face. "Thank you, Jeremy. Thank you. You are the best brother in the world. This is wonderful! Oh, thank you." With that, she ran back to Richard and hugged him tightly. "Oh, Richard, this is so wonderful. It's a good thing I have some plans already made. I shall finish the details right away. I think we should get married next month or perhaps July. No, I guess late June before we leave."

"What do you mean 'before you leave'?" Jeremy asked. "You mean on a wedding trip?"

"You didn't tell him, Richard."

"Tell me what?"

"I didn't get the opportunity to tell him, Catherine. You jumped in before I was finished, remember?"

Richard came back to the table and sat down. "Jeremy, I'm thinking of going to the Americas. I've heard so much about it. All the reports are it's exciting and wonderful and you can have your own land, too, free for the taking. I'm young and strong and I love a challenge. I think I could do very well there."

Several emotions flitted across Jeremy's face as thoughts whirled through his mind. "I've heard it's very dangerous in the New World, Richard. It's a wild country, uncivilized."

"But think of the adventure, the opportunities that will present themselves as it becomes more settled. I want to be part of that, Jeremy. Because of our different stations in life, perhaps you do not realize what this means to me. It is freedom."

"Freedom?! I didn't realize you regarded yourself as a slave, Richard," Jeremy said stiffly.

"I don't think of myself as a slave. You and your parents before you, always made me feel like part of your family, Jeremy. But that's the point. This is your house, your family. I want to establish my own family and way of life."

"Wait a minute. You mean you are thinking of taking Catherine there?"

"I want to go, Jeremy. I feel just like Richard. It will be a fantastic adventure and fun. I realize there will be hardships, but I'm strong and I don't mind. And Richard will be there to take care of me." Catherine looked steadily at Jeremy. "I know you think I'm still a baby and silly sometimes, but Jemmy, I am being most serious now when I tell you I love Richard dearly. I want to spend the rest of my life with him and if he goes to America, I will go with him."

Jeremy regarded Catherine's earnest face. "I'd like to think about this for a while. Exactly when were you thinking of leaving?"

"After our wedding, perhaps July."

"No! Absolutely not July, Richard."

"But why? Why not July?"

"Look, I have asked you to let me think about it, all right? Give me some time to get used to the idea and work things out. There are ... there is unrest in London. Please. You must do this for me."

"Oh very well, but I am going to finish making wedding plans. I can't just do this overnight, you know," said Catherine.

Jeremy smiled. "All right, you impatient girl. Go ahead and make your wedding plans. Just postpone the notion of America for now."

Chapter 30

Hawkesbury Manor, May 1588

Lying in his bed that night, Jeremy thought of his sister and Richard, America, Spain, his brother, England and danger, until his mind was a maelstrom that threatened to keep him awake all night. At last he fell into a troubled sleep, full of shadows and light, and strange beasts rising out of deep waters. Toward morning, he awoke with a start and realized somewhere in the torment of his dreams, decisions had been made. Jeremy pulled himself out of bed and by the time Richard arrived, was already sitting in his special chair.

"You're certainly up early, Jeremy." Richard said as he stoked the fire to take the chill out of the air.

"I am indeed and just waiting for your leaden footfalls, my friend," Jeremy said with a tired smile. "I didn't sleep well last night thinking of what you asked me yesterday, but when I woke this morning, I realized nothing would be nicer for me than to have you as a brother-in-law. Incidentally, have you told your mother yet?"

"No. We thought we wanted to discuss this with you first."

"I think this should make owl-face very happy. She has always felt you should be lord of the manor. I'm not too sure how she will take to the idea of you leaving for America though."

"I don't really care what ... wait! What did you say?"

"I said I didn't think your mother would be too pleased to have you and Catherine leave for America."

Richard beamed. "You mean it? You agree? We have your blessing to go?"

"With one condition. You must not set sail until next year."

"But why? We would like to go soon after the wedding."

"I cannot really explain why to you, Richard, except to say it will be much safer then. You will have to trust me on this. That is my decision and it is not open for bartering. Do you agree to this one condition?"

Richard regarded his friend steadfastly. He knew Jeremy was not given to whimsies. "This is the only way?"

"Yes. There can be no other."

"Then I agree and thank you, Jeremy. You may rest assured I will always take very good care of Catherine. I am eternally grateful to you."

"I hope you still feel that way after you are married and Catherine starts ordering you about." Jeremy laughed.

"After we are married?? She already orders me about. But it is with a feather whip and I don't mind in the least."

John laughed again at Richard's besotted countenance. "You are smitten. I wish both of you the best of good fortune. You had better go tell Catherine if she is about."

"Oh, do you mind?" Richard asked eagerly. "I'll be very quick. Is there anything I can do for you," he continued, backing into a chair and nearly toppling it.

"Yes. You can get out of here before you destroy my room."

"I'm gone."

Jeremy smiled as he gazed out at the cloudy morning. "I hope I have done the right thing."

The next few weeks passed quickly as the household became a flurry of activity, cleaning and cooking for the planned nuptials.

With both her parents dead, Catherine had a free hand in making all the arrangements, and on a glorious day late in June, she and Richard were married, with everything going smoothly according to Catherine's well-organized plans. John had been invited but had declined due, he said, to ill health - a ruse which fooled everyone but Jeremy. Catherine had momentarily thought to postpone her marriage, but the day had almost arrived by the time she heard from John, and Jeremy encouraged her to go ahead.

As time passed and his other life became more distant, Jeremy relaxed, for it appeared he had succeeded in hiding his identity from Parker, Brooks and the Spaniard, Vasquez. John had sent a private message stating he would be commanding a ship in the fleet which would defend England from the invaders. Also included were personal thanks from Queen Elizabeth for Jeremy's part in uncovering the conspiracy.

While Richard and Catherine were wrapped up in their own blissful world, Jeremy thought of beautiful, generous Meggie, and wondered if he would ever see her again. He anxiously awaited word of the battle which he knew must be taking place. Rumors and stories were circulating throughout the country, but it wasn't until a newsbook arrived in December with a full account of the whole battle, that all the details were known to those at Hawkesbury Hall.

According to the newsbook, the Duke of Sedonia and his Armada had reached the southwest coast of England only to find themselves challenged and harassed by the English fleet, who avoided the close-in combat desired by the Spanish. The Armada had sailed up the English Channel, where the English ships continued to bombard them, until the Spanish turned back and anchored at Calais. The Duke of Parma had failed to meet them, and the English took this opportunity to attack the Spanish fleet with fire-ships. An eight hour struggle ensued during the Battle of Gravelines and ended with many Spanish ships lost or damaged.

The Duke of Sedonia decided to give up on his attempted invasion and return to Spain via the north of Scotland and Ireland, but the English fleet had pursued the Spanish into the North Sea, returning home only when they ran out of ammunition. Many of the Armada ships were sunk by storms off the coasts of Scotland and Ireland, and those that survived returned to Spain crushed and dejected.

There was no mention of the Catholic rebels who had intended to join the Spanish troops when they landed in England. Jeremy guessed they must have decided to keep their plans secret until such times as the soldiers actually arrived.

The newsbook went on to relate the Queen had gone for a walk among the people of London and ultimately gave a speech where she stated quite forcefully she would not fear anyone trying to invade England and she believed her subjects to be a "faithful and loving people", and assuring everyone England would be victorious over anyone who dared to try and invade her beloved country.

Following on the heels of the story in the newsbook was a message from John relating the celebrations taking place in London. Lord Howard, Francis Drake and the men who had fought so valiantly under them, were being treated to well-deserved, lavish feasts.

Jeremy was gratified at his brother's kind words. "It is a pity you cannot be acknowledged, my brother, for without your assistance, we would be under Spanish rule and there would be little celebration in the land. You are the true hero of this whole battle and I wish everyone could know, but I realize this would place you in grave danger. There are still traitors in our midst, Jeremy, and you must always keep a watchful eye. Please give my love to Catherine and Richard. It is unlikely I shall see any of you in the near future, as Francis has confided in me I will be sailing with him in the new year, to where, of course, I cannot say. May God be with you, Jeremy. Your loving brother, John."

"Traitors in our midst," murmured Jeremy as he gazed at the gray December skies. "Indeed there will always be traitors as long as there are causes. I wonder if the New World is plagued with traitors." For some time, he had been contemplating the idea of venturing to America, trying to visualize what it would be like, wondering if he would survive the long sea journey and, most important, would Meggie want to go with him. The thought of a future without her seemed very bleak.

Christmas came and went, and although Catherine and Richard did their best to entertain Jeremy, he slumped into a deep depression, increased by the very merriment with which they sought to cheer him.

Finally in late February, he told them what was troubling him. "While I was away, I met a lovely girl named Meggie. We were both attracted to each other, nay, more than that - we fell in love."

"Why Jeremy, that's wonderful!" exclaimed Catherine. "But why didn't you invite her to our wedding? She could have come here and ..."

"Wait a moment, Catherine. For reasons I can't explain to you, it was impossible for me to invite her to your wedding or contact her in any way. I did promise her I would come back to see her within a year and the time is approaching. Part of the problem is, I am not sure if she would really want to share her future with a ... a cripple. She is a beautiful girl and any man would be lucky to have her for a wife." He looked forlornly out the window.

Catherine put her hands on her hips. "Any woman would be lucky to have you for a husband," she stated emphatically.

"I agree with that," said Richard, crossing his legs.

Catherine's interest was piqued. "Where does she live?"

"In Tiddlebury, which is not too far from London. Her father owns the tavern there."

"Tiddlebury! How in the world did you come to meet her if you were in Edinburgh?!" Catherine said.

"I'm afraid that will have to remain one of life's little mysteries, Catherine. Let's just say I spent a bit of time there ... long enough for us to fall in love."

"I think it's wonderful you met someone, Jeremy, no matter how," said Richard, jumping to his feet.

"I do too, and I can't wait to meet her." Catherine grabbed Jeremy's arms. "Will you be married here? Please say yes, so I can plan it all for you, please Jemmy?"

Jeremy laughed. "I could hardly resist such a heartfelt plea, now could I, Catherine?"

Catherine clapped her hands and danced in place. "I shall start right away. When would you like it to happen?"

"I think probably June, but I'll let you know after I talk to Meggie."

"Be quick about it, then. I can hardly wait," Catherine said, grabbing Richard and dancing around the room. "It will be such fun!"

"There's something else. Ever since you told me about going to America, I have been thinking about joining you." Catherine stopped so quickly, she stumbled into Richard. "There are reasons why this might be a very good move for me, but I am not sure if Meggie would want to come with me."

Richard and Catherine exchanged astonished looks.

"You wouldn't mind if I went, would you?" said Jeremy, watching their reaction. "It's not as though we would have to stay together when we get there if you prefer to be alone."

"Mind??!!" exclaimed Catherine, running over and throwing her arms around her brother. "You silly goose, of course we wouldn't mind. We're just so ... so ..."

"Amazed," said Richard. "Never in a million years did I think you would consider leaving Hawkesbury to go anywhere, let alone the New World. And Catherine's right. We would really be happy if you were with us." He shook Jeremy's hand. "Don't even entertain the notion of separating after arrival. When do you think we might leave?"

"Perhaps June or July. Obviously you did a wonderful job of inspiring me about the adventure of going to America. I only hope I will fare as well in my talk with Meggie."

"If Meggie has half a brain in her head, she will jump at the opportunity to be with you, Jeremy. Will you be going to call on her? Perhaps I could go with you," said Catherine eagerly.

"Yes and no. I will call on her, but it is best if I go alone. I really think this is something I must do in person. In fact, I will leave on the morrow, now that I know you are agreeable to my plans."

"Would you like me to come with you?"

"Thank you, Richard, but no. I shall go alone."

"As you wish."

Chapter 31

The Crown & Anchor, April 1589

In the gray misty dawn, Jeremy once more set forth on a journey to Tiddlebury, but this time with a far different purpose. He arrived at the Crown and Anchor a few nights later, and finding no one in the stable, took the carriage around to the front of the building. A passerby agreed to go inside and inquire for Mr. McIntosh and moments later, Ian appeared, bringing a waft of the familiar tavern smells with him.

"What's this all about now," he called, peering in the dimness.

"Ian, good man. It is I, Thomas Smithson."

"Who? What?" Coming closer, he saw Jeremy's face. "Bless me! I don't believe it! Thomas, is it really you? How are ye laddie?" Ian energetically grabbed Jeremy's hand. "Pleased I am to see you. The missus will be too. Ach, it's a good job she's not here or she'd be after askin' me why I'm keeping you out in the cold."

"Are there many people inside?"

"No, and those that are be too drunk to see their own hands. Come on, round the back, laddie." Ian took hold of the horse's bridle and led them to the back of the tavern.

"Grab your bag and I'll carry you in. Have you got your chair with you?"

"Yes, in back."

"I'll get it after I get you safely inside."

"How is your dear wife? In good health, I hope?

"Aye, she's just fine. She'll be right pleased to see you, too."

"I wonder if I might have a word with the two of you, Ian, once we get in."

"Of course, laddie. Nancy's in the kitchen. Did you want to talk to us now?"

"Yes, please, if you have a minute."

With a seemingly effortless motion, Ian hoisted Jeremy over his shoulders and carried him into the steamy room.

"Who's this you're bringing in my kitchen, Mr. McIntosh?"

As Ian put Jeremy into a chair, Nancy grabbed her breast. "Glory be to heaven! If it isn't young Thomas!"

"Wonderful to see you, Nancy. Come give me a hug."

Ian sat down while Mrs. McIntosh did as requested. She drew back and held his face in her hands. "My, but it's wonderful to see you again, Thomas. Are you here for a long stay?"

"That depends on whether or not you and Mr. McIntosh toss me out on my ear after hearing what I have to say."

The couple looked at each other.

"I cannot imagine anything you might say that would make us throw you out, laddie," Ian said.

"I sincerely hope not." Jeremy smiled. "I've come to ask you for Meggie's hand in marriage."

Mrs. McIntosh beamed. "I told you so, Ian! I knew they was in love with each other. I knew it!"

Jeremy laughed. "Was it that obvious?"

"A mother knows these things," Nancy said, smiling.

"I'm sure we'd be pleased to have you for a son, laddie. You have our blessing, right Mrs. McIntosh?"

"Indeed. Yes, indeed."

"Now I'll have to see if Meggie will have me. Is she here?"

"Aye. She's helping in the tavern. Why don't I take you in there, then I'll bring in your chair." Ian rose and came to Jeremy.

"That would be fine. Thank you, Ian."

Ian carried Jeremy into the pub and sat him at a table near the back. Meggie was busy delivering ale to a table of four when Ian spoke to her. Her face lit up and she rushed over, skirts flying, face flushed.

"Thomas! Oh, Thomas. I can't believe you're really here. I was beginning to think I'd never see you again." She leaned over and hugged him.

"Meggie, darling." He took her hand and kissed it. "Meggie, I promised to return. I've missed you so much. I have lived for the past year on the memories of our last night. We have much to talk about."

"But not here, Thomas," she said, waving her arm to indicate all the people. "You'll have to wait till I've finished me work. If you're staying here, I'll come to your room when I'm done."

"I am staying here. I expect it will be the same room as before."

"Oh, it's so wonderful to see you. Are you thirsty after your trip? Would you want a drink, love?"

"Yes, please."

Meggie smiled and went off to the bar.

Jeremy looked around and tried to visualize how different things would be if last year's battle had been won by the other side. His reverie was interrupted by a familiar young voice speaking loudly beside him. "Master Thomas! Is that really you?"

Startled, Jeremy drew back from the face peering at him only a few inches from his own.

"Crikey, yer don't look half different, Master Thomas, what with no beard and all." Round eyes reflected his astonishment. "It's me, Adam. Remember? Mr. McIntosh told me to see to yer 'orse, and I just wanted to pay me respects, but I can't believe how you look."

Jeremy looked around quickly, but no one appeared to be paying any attention. "Of course, I remember you, Adam. How are you?"

"Just fine, thank'ee, Master Thomas. Well, I'd best be off to tend to yer 'orse afore Mr. McIntosh starts hollerin.'"

Mumbling and shaking his head, Adam made his way through the room to the back door.

Jeremy watched Adam's progress until he was interrupted by the arrival of Meggie with his ale. As she leaned over to place it in front of him, the sight of her soft white bosom flooded Jeremy's mind with memories of candlelight flickering on her naked body.

"There you go." Meggie squeezed his arm affectionately. "I've got to help Dad get ready to close, but I'll come to see you as soon as I can."

"That's fine, darling."

After all the patrons had gone, Ian hurried over to carry Jeremy to his room, followed closely by Meggie and her mother who appeared from the kitchen carrying a laden tray.

"Here ye are - some nice sweets to go with your tea," Nancy said, putting the tray in front of Meggie.

"Why thank you, Nancy. That's very nice of you," Jeremy said taking her hand and kissing it. "You are still my favourite girl."

"Away with ye, and in front of your betrothed too! Just call if you need anything, Thomas. Mr. McIntosh, I need help in the kitchen," Nancy said, taking Ian by the arm.

"But I thought I could visit for a minute," he protested.

"You can do your visiting tomorrow. Come with me now," Nancy said, shooing her husband to the door and closing it firmly behind her.

The young couple laughed. "I think your mother is a romantic at heart," Jeremy said.

"I think you're right." She kissed Jeremy quickly and then poured the tea. "I'm uncomfortable with Mommy waiting on me," Meggie began, "and why did she say 'betrothed?'"

"Because she and your Dad gave me permission to ask you to marry me." He took hold of her hands. "I love you with all my heart,

Meggie. Do you still want to marry me and share the rest of our lives together?" He searched her face.

"Oh yes! I would like nothing more than to marry you and be with you forever," she said, kissing his hands.

"Are you sure you want to marry someone like this?" Jeremy said, nodding to his legs.

"Oh love. I never even think about those. It is the darling person who lives inside that I love. Of course, I want to marry you." She sat on his lap and rubbed her cheek on his.

"As to being uncomfortable by someone waiting on you, well, you'll just have to get used to it if you're going to be Mrs. Jeremy Hawkins."

Meggie sat back and stared at him. "Who? What?"

"My real name is Jeremy Hawkins. I couldn't tell you that before. So, if you marry me, you will be Mrs. Jeremy Hawkins."

"Mrs. Jeremy Hawkins. Meggie Hawkins. Oooh, I like the sound of that." She threw her arms around Jeremy and kissed him. "But I thought you were ... why did you tell us you were Thomas Smithson?"

"I'm afraid I can't tell you, Meggie, other than to say I couldn't be here under my real name. Please just trust me on this, all right?"

"You know I trust you."

He kissed her briefly. "Then there is just one more thing to do. I'm sorry I cannot get down on my knees for the official asking." Jeremy pulled a velvet bag from his pocket and removed a ring. Jeremy extended it toward Meggie and said, "Meggie McIntosh, will you do me the honour of becoming my wife?"

"Yes, Jeremy Hawkins, with all my heart I wish nothing more than to be your wife."

Jeremy slipped the ring on her finger. Meggie gazed in awe as the large red ruby and circlet of large diamonds sparkled in the light.

She drew in her breath. "This ring is so beautiful, Jeremy."

"Not nearly as beautiful as you, love."

They kissed again, hungrily this time, their tongues intertwining. They moved slightly apart, pulling in deep breaths.

"I have another proposition for you, Meggie. My sister Catherine married Richard Pedley last year and they have decided to go to America to live. I would like us to go with them as husband and wife." Jeremy paused when he saw Meggie's shocked face.

"America!" Meggie said, with a sigh of wonder. "I've never been anywhere but Tiddlebury."

"My dear heart, if you don't want to, then we won't."

"Don't want to??!! Does the Queen not want to live in her palace?!" Meggie jumped up, her eyes sparkling. "Of course I want to go. Just imagine! Me in America." She twirled around, arm extended, admiring her ring. "My friends won't be half jealous." Throwing her arms around Jeremy, she continued, "When are we going?"

"This summer, likely June, on the first ship we can get. Oh, Meggie, are you sure about this?"

"I'm sure. I'm sure. I'm sure," she cried, covering Jeremy's face with kisses. "But what about our wedding? How am I ... where ...?"

"Don't worry your pretty head about the wedding. Catherine has offered to make all the arrangements at Hawkesbury."

"Are you sure she won't mind?"

"Mind? She is in her glory. She did her own last year and is delighted to plan another one for us. Hopefully my brother John will be able to come, although he's most times out to sea. I'll call on him before I go home to find out."

"You have a brother who's a sailor?"

"Yes. John Hawkins. He's a captain and often goes on voyages with Drake. I'd rather you didn't talk to anyone about that though, dearest."

"Why not?"

"Again, I can't say. Can your heart trust me on this, too, sweetheart?"

"Certainly, love."

"Perhaps you would like to come to Hawkesbury now so you and Catherine can talk about dresses and whatever it is that women need to talk about for weddings."

Meggie dropped into a chair. "But my job here? My parents? Daddy needs time to find a replacement for me in the tavern."

"I think your parents expect you to leave here, although perhaps not as far as America. But they know I'll take care of you, dearest."

"And I have things to do, Jeremy, and no doubt Mom and Dad will want to have a party."

"Please forgive my wanting to hurry. You are right, of course, and we must give Catherine time to get our wedding organized, so why don't we plan on leaving in a few weeks when everything here is settled?"

"Oh, Thomas ...um... Jeremy, that sounds perfect. I will trust Catherine to make all the wedding preparations, if you're sure she won't mind."

"She will be happy to do that."

"Good. Then I will get my dress here and we should be ready to leave near the end of May."

"That's two months!" Jeremy sighed. "I don't know if I can wait that long."

Meggie laughed. "Well, you will just have to. Arranging all this takes time, you know. You can't expect it to happen overnight."

"You win. I will be patient. Perhaps we will be able to arrange a short visit with John if he's home. I would love to have him to meet you."

"It will be wonderful to meet your family, Jeremy."

"They will welcome you warmly. I do love you so much, Meggie."

"And I, you, my impatient darling." Meggie jumped to her feet. "I don't think it's all got through my head yet. Can I go tell Mother and Father?"

Jeremy laughed at Meggie's excitement. "Go on, then. Better break it gently though, especially the part about America."

"I will. Don't worry. They'll be very happy for me, I know."

Meggie kissed him hard and raced to the door. She turned swiftly back to Jeremy. "I'm not dreaming, am I, Jeremy Hawkins?"

"You are wide awake, I assure you."

Meggie flew back to Jeremy's arms. "Oh Jeremy, I love you so much. You're my whole world."

"You're mine too, Meggie. You have made me the happiest man alive. Now get, before you explode."

Meggie gave him a wave from the door, almost closed it, leaned back in to blow him a kiss, and with a final wave, shut the door and scurried down the hall.

Smiling to himself, Jeremy completed his preparations and gratefully sank into his bed. Exhaustion overcame him and he fell into a deep, contented sleep.

Chapter 32

Madrid, Spain, Late April 1589

Since his return from his latest audience with Philip II, General Perez was angrier than David Lancaster had ever seen him. David watched him pacing up and down, his face growing redder by the minute.

"Me! They think I must know who revealed the Armada plans to the English. Me! The most loyal of Spaniards. And do you know why? Because I have an English son-in-law. God forgive me for ever allowing Isabella to marry you." He whirled around. "And now ... " he lowered his voice threateningly. "Do you know what I think now??!! YOU! You were a spy for that witch on the throne of England. You are the one who betrayed us."

David blanched. "No sir, of course I wasn't. I was here with my lovely Isabella the whole time. She will tell you."

"Phfft! A woman will say anything when she's in love! I know you were in England two years ago." The General's face was inches from David's and his eyes burned with suspicion. "Did you agree to spy for them?"

"No sir. I assure you I did not. My loyalties now lie with you, good King Philip and Spain."

"But perhaps you know someone who might have been spying." David wondered for a few seconds if Jeremy had disregarded his warning. His momentary hesitation was not lost on the General. "AHA! There is someone!" The General's beefy hand grabbed David's lapels. "Who is it? Tell me now!"

"There is a man ... he spied for Elizabeth before. Perhaps he may have done so again. I don't know for certain."

"His name!" David hesitated again. "His NAME!" The General shook David, nearly pulling him off his feet.

"Jeremy Hawkins."

"Hawkins?? Is he related to that scoundrel, John Hawkins?"

"Yes, they are brothers."

"Madre de Dios! I might have guessed it. And where does this person live?"

David recoiled from the spittle that hit his face. "In Nottinghamshire."

"Where did this spying take place and where is he now?"

"I don't know. I swear. I don't know."

The General released David and shoved him backwards. "Then you will find out. Go to England." Perez pulled the bell cord. "Vasquez will accompany you, and you will let him know. He will take care of things from there."

David was straightening his clothes when Vasquez came into the room.

"You will accompany Lancaster to England. When he finds out where the spy is, you know what to do, Vasquez. Do not return until he has been eliminated, do you understand?"

"Si, General Perez. It shall be as you wish." Vasquez turned to David. "Are you ready?"

"I have to pack and say goodbye to my wife."

"Be quick about it. I want you out of here in half an hour," Perez said.

David Lancaster drew a deep breath. "As you wish."

Four days later under cover of darkness, Vasquez and Lancaster were brought ashore in a small bay in southeast England. Brooks met them at the wharf and escorted them to Parker's house.

Vasquez wrinkled his nose at the stale smells of tobacco and food, and dusted off a chair before sitting down.

"Who's this, then?" Parker said, nodding toward Lancaster.

"Someone who is going to help us get rid of the bastard who gave away our plans. Whoever he is must have been at the Crown & Anchor when we were discussing the plans," Brooks said. "Do you have a name?"

"I have a name who's a possibility, but I don't know where he is at the moment," said Lancaster.

"The plan is for David to go to his home and if he is there, to lure him away so you two can take care of him," Vasquez said. "If he is not there, he will find out where he is, and you will go to that place. There are to be no mistakes, you understand? He is to be disposed of."

Parker nodded his head emphatically. "I'll take care of the rotter. Yer can count on me and me boys."

"There will be no mistake," Brooks said. "When do you want to leave?"

"First thing in the morning, I would think," said David. "It will take us a day to get close by. We'll stay overnight at an inn, and I'll go to his place the next day."

"I ain't got money to pay for no inn, thanks to that rat," said Parker. "Who's gonna pay for it?"

Vasquez looked distastefully at Parker. "I'm sure we can take care of your needs. Where is the closest inn to here? We should retire soon so we can get an early start tomorrow."

"You can stay at my house," said Brooks. "My wife is away visiting her family, and it will be safer there than at an inn."

"That sounds fine, thank you," David said before Vasquez could object.

Their plans were completed as decided, and just before noon, David Lancaster rode a horse up to the door of Hawkesbury Manor.

As she happened to be close by, Mrs. Pedley opened the door. Much happier now in her elevated position of mother-in-law, she smiled at the visitor. "Mr. Lancaster! What a surprise! How nice to see you."

"Ah, Mrs. P., looking beautiful as always. Come give us a kiss."

"Mr. Lancaster, shame on you. And you a married man and all. Please come in."

David laughed. "Is Jeremy about?"

"No, I'm afraid he's not."

"Who's at the door," Catherine said coming down the hallway. "Oh David! How wonderful to see you. Come in, come in. It's been such a long time. Is your wife with you?" she said, looking over his shoulder.

"No, I'm by myself."

"No matter. Come and sit down. Would you like tea? Mrs. Pedley, would you mind asking Mrs. Stewart to make up a tea tray, and please feel free to join us, if you wish."

David followed Catherine into the sitting-room. "You've turned into quite a young lady since I last saw you, Catherine."

"Actually, I am a married woman now, David. Please sit down."

"Thank you. And who is the lucky man?"

"You remember Richard Pedley? He and I were married last year."

"Congratulations then." He came over and kissed her on the cheek. "That explains why you invited Mrs. Pedley to tea."

"Yes, she's my mother-in-law now. Not only that, but Jemmy is getting married soon."

"Getting married? When?"

"I'm not exactly sure, but likely June."

Mrs. Pedley arrived with a tea tray. She set it down but excused herself from staying, saying that she was having some difficulty in training the new housekeeper. Catherine thanked her and poured two cups.

"So you were talking about Jeremy getting married. When is that to be?"

She handed a cup to David. "I'm not sure. We'll know when he gets back with his fiancee."

"Gets back? His fiancee isn't from around here I gather."

"No, he met her last year when he was away in Edinburgh."

David tried not to appear too eager. "Really. Edinburgh?" He took a sip of his tea. "So, uh, I supposed that's where he's gone now."

"Oh no. Meggie doesn't live there. Her father owns a tavern in Tiddlebury, just outside London, so Jeremy said."

"I see. I suppose you're looking forward to meeting the young lady ... soon, I imagine." He cleared his throat. "And when are they likely to come back here?"

"I've no idea. I'm just making plans for their wedding, to be prepared for whenever they arrive. Perhaps you would like to stay on for the wedding. I know Jemmy would love to see you."

"Unfortunately, that's not possible, Catherine. I ... uh ... I have to get back to Spain right away. My wife - you know how it is - she doesn't like to be alone for too long." David tipped up his cup and looked at Catherine as he replaced it on the saucer. "So, uh, perhaps Jeremy's in Tiddlebury now?"

"I would think so. I'm sure the young lady, whose name is Meggie, by the way, has things to do before coming here."

"No doubt," David said, putting down his cup and saucer on the tray. "Catherine, I'm sorry to cut my visit short, but I have to meet someone and I'll be late if I don't leave now. I just wanted to stop by to see you and Jeremy." He stood up. "Thank you for your hospitality, and very best wishes for a happy future with Richard."

"Thank you, David. Jeremy will be sorry he missed you. I'll tell him you came by though."

David kissed her on the cheek, mounted his horse and rode off in such a hurry, he didn't see Catherine's wave goodbye, or the slightly puzzled look on her face.

Chapter 33

The Crown & Anchor, Late May 1589

Adam ran out to meet the coach as it pulled to a stop behind the tavern. "Pleased I am to see you back, Miss Meggie and Master Jeremy," he said while reaching up to remove Jeremy's chair.

"Thank you, Adam. We're pleased to be back," Jeremy said.

"I'll just be a minute gettin' Mr. McIntosh," Adam said, dashing inside.

"We had such a lovely visit with your brother, Jeremy. What a gentle soul he is, not what I expected from a seafaring man."

"I believe he rules with a velvet glove and his men love him for it. Very loyal they are, always waiting to go with him on the next voyage."

"So you're back." Ian said, settling Jeremy in his wheeled chair. "How was your trip?"

Meggie gave her father a kiss. "It was very nice. Jeremy's brother is a real sweetheart."

"A sweetheart, is he? Maybe it's him you should be marrying then." Ian laughed and slapped Jeremy on the shoulder.

"Not a chance," said Meggie. "Jeremy's the man I love."

"We've been missing you," Ian McIntosh said.

Meggie kissed her father again. "Better get used to it, Daddy. We'll be leaving again very shortly. But not before you come to our wedding."

"We'll be doing that, daughter. You can count on it. Meanwhile, your mother's been busy making arrangements for a big party for the two of you before we all head off to Jeremy's place. And speaking of your mother ... she's covering the bar. I'd better get in there to help out before she rebels."

Mrs. McIntosh spied them as they came into the main room and hurried over through the patrons, arms outstretched. "My lovies. Back from your trip, and mighty happy am I to see you both." She gave each of them a hug in turn. "Mr. McIntosh, you'd best be seeing to your customers. They're a thirsty bunch tonight."

"Just like any other," Ian said, taking his place behind the counter.

Adam came rushing in. "I got yer bags put in yer room, Master Jeremy and yours, too, Miss Meggie."

"Thank you, Adam."

"My pleasure, sir. Now I must see to yon horse." Adam beamed, then hurried away.

"I'll come and help you, Daddy, as soon as I get unpacked."

"No rush. Just hurry up," said Ian with a smile.

"Wonderful it is to have you home," said Nancy. "I'd best get me to the kitchen. There's some orders to fill."

From a dark corner, the cold eyes of Seth Parker watched the three of them leave. Scowling, he rose to his feet, exited out the back door into the laneway, crossed to the stable and following the noises, found Adam grooming Jeremy's chestnut mare.

"Nice 'orse. She yers?"

Adam jumped. "Yer scared me, sir. Didn't hear you comin."' He patted the horse and continued, "This here 'orse ain't mine. I'm just in charge of her while Master Jeremy is here."

"That the bloke I saw yer talkin' ter in the Crown? Looked familiar. Think I seen 'im 'ere a while back. He don't quite look the same."

"Crikey, he don't half look diff'runt. That's what I said. I mean he got rid of that big beard and all. Looks a proper gentleman now 'e does."

"What be 'is last name? It's kinda slipped me mind," Parker said with a friendly smile.

"Smithson it was, but it's really Hawkins. He be a friend of Captain 'awkins what fought against them Spanish last year. Quite famous, he is. The Captain, I mean." Adam rattled on, proud to boast of his association with the upper class. "I even got to go to his 'ouse once with a very important message."

Adam stopped, a look of doubt crossing his face as he recalled the secrecy of his mission. He shrugged off the thought, deciding time had somehow erased the necessity. Wishing to add to his importance, Adam exaggerated a little and said, "Talked to him myself, I did."

"A message, you say?"

Adam lowered his voice. "A secret message. The fate of England was in me hands. He told me so."

"Yer must be a right important feller and pleased I am ter 'ave been talkin' to you. I've got to be pushing off. Me buddies are waitin' fer me. Yer keep on working with that 'orse. Yer doin' a fine job."

"Aye, I will. Thankee, sir." Adam watched the stranger leave. "Nice chap," he said to the horse. "Maybe I should tell Master Jeremy his friend was asking for him. You've got yer feed to keep you happy till I get back," he said, patting the horse on the rump.

Adam hurried back to the tavern and inside where he ran into the bulky form of Mrs. McIntosh carrying a tray of food.

"Whist, laddie. And where do you think you're off to?"

"I've just got to tell Master Jeremy something."

"Did his horse drop dead?"

Adam was shocked. He shook his head. "Oh no, Missus. Never!"

"Well, then, ye'll no bother him now. He's got company in his room, and he doesn't need the likes of you barging in there. Away with you. You can tell him tomorrow. Now, go. Go!"

Crestfallen, Adam turned and disappeared out the door.

Muttering to herself, Nancy continued on to Jeremy's room. "I've made you both a bite to eat, seeing as you missed supper."

"Thank you, Nancy. That's very kind of you."

"I'll eat quickly, so I can go help Daddy," Meggie said, taking the tray from her mother.

"Don't be givin' yourself indigestion, Meggie. He'll be closing up in a couple of hours anyway. Take your time. And both of you should get a good sleep tonight, because we'll be wanting to hear all about your trip and what's going on in London these days."

"Goodnight, Nancy. I'll be happy to turn in a bit early," Jeremy said.

"I'll bring the tray back when we're done, Mommy."

"Your parents are so kind, Meggie. I am very lucky to have found not only a beautiful woman who loves me, but a wonderful family who have welcomed me like a son. I am a blessed man in this lifetime. I hope I will be as fortunate in my next," Jeremy said, helping himself to a scone.

"Well, please don't be in a big hurry to get to your next life, love. I'd like to spend a lot of years together with you before you depart this life," Meggie said, with a smile.

"You will, my darling. We shall have a multitude of children, grow old and fat together, and bounce grandchildren on our knees." Jeremy laughed before biting into his scone.

"If I'm going to get fat, I hope you will still love me then," said Meggie.

Jemmy brought her hand to his lips and kissed it. Looking deep into her eyes, he said, "I will love you always, Meggie, for the rest of our lives in this world and right into the next. You can count on that."

"All right then. I won't worry about getting fat." Meggie laughed aloud. "Now eat your supper so I can get this tray back to the kitchen."

"Yes, ma'am. Whatever you say." Jeremy laughed with her. "I have to finish quickly as I have been ordered to get to sleep early. The women in this house seem to rule the men."

"Of course. Isn't that the way things are supposed to be?"

"So it is in my world, anyway."

They both laughed as if it were the funniest thing they'd ever heard.

Chapter 34

The Crown & Anchor, Late May 1589

Jeremy was rudely awakened about three in the morning as rough hands yanked him out of bed and onto the floor in one swift movement. Jeremy's arms were tied behind his back and a gag knotted securely over his mouth. Two of the men carried him silently into the hall and out the back door. They dragged him to a small shack several yards from the stables and dumped him on the floor.

One of the men lit a candle and brought his scarred face close to Jeremy's. "Remember me, yer lordship? Yer ought to. Yer seen me oft enough."

The smell of Parker's breath was nauseating and Jeremy turned his head away.

Parker grabbed a fistful of Jeremy's hair and yanked his head around. "Don't yer want to look at me? Yer looked at me last year, didn't you? Listened to me and Brooks makin' plans." He slapped Jeremy hard in the face.

"Hold 'im up," Parker ordered the two men with him. "Yer can't even stand like a man, but yer caused me all kinds of trouble, you slimy eel. Yer the one what warned them others, ain'tcher." Ben Parker hit Jeremy hard in the stomach. Jeremy doubled over but the thugs yanked him up by his hair "I didn't get me money on account of you." Parker hit him again. Jeremy groaned.

"They all got mad at me." A big beefy hand thudded against Jeremy's jaw, causing bone to crunch and blood to spurt out from his nose.

Parker untied the gag from Jeremy's mouth and threw the filthy rag aside. "Wouldn't want you stranglin' on yer blood afore I gets done with you." He landed another blow on Jeremy's face, opening a cut across his left eye. Jeremy grunted and passed out. The two men dropped his sagging body to the floor.

"Bastard," Parker said, kicking Jeremy's back with his heavy boots. "I'll show you. Sit 'im in that chair, boys. Looks like we'll have to wake 'im up. Tiny, fetch me some water from the stable and be quick about it. Willy, tie his chest to the chair so he don't fall off."

All 300 pounds of Tiny came back with a pail of water which Parker threw into Jeremy's face. "Wake up, ye bugger, I ain't done yet. Protestant pig, give me away, would you? I'm going to fix it so you never tell anybody anything again."

Through water and blood, Jeremy dimly saw his tormenters. As Parker drew back to swing again, Tiny caught his arm. "Hold on. What about us? How come we don't get any of the fun? It were our money too."

"All right. Have a go." Parker stood aside.

Jeremy closed his eyes as he saw Tiny's huge fist coming toward his face. The force of the blow caused the chair to topple over and break into several pieces.

"Here's an idea," said Willy, picking up a piece of the chair and hitting Jeremy with such force that his body bounced. The other two followed suit and beat Jeremy with all the strength they could muster.

"Hold on lads. I ain't half worn out." Parker wiped the sweat off his face and looked at Jeremy's inert body. "I think he's dead anyways. Ain't no fun if he can't feel it."

As Tiny raised his stick for a final blow, Willy stayed his arm. "Shhhh. Someone's comin'. Let's git." The three men moved swiftly out of the shack and were swallowed up by the darkness.

Stealing slowly along the outside of the building, wide eyes peering cautiously as he moved his lantern from side to side, Adam called, "Is someone there?"

At the door of the shack, Adam paused and carefully looked inside. "Hello?"

To his horror, the lantern light picked up a body crumpled on the floor. "Oh, my gawd!" In trepidation, Adam crept closer, till his lantern finally revealed Jeremy's battered face. He drew back quickly and, panic-stricken, ran out the door and back to the tavern.

"Mr. McIntosh! Mr. McIntosh! Wake up!" Adam cried from the laneway. "Mr. McIntosh! Help!"

An upstairs window opened and Ian poked his head out, with Nancy looking over his shoulder. "What's all the hollerin' about? Is that you, Adam?"

"Aye. You've got to come! It's Master Jeremy. He's been hurt. I think he's dead."

"What?!"

"Whist man, are ye deaf? He said Master Jeremy's hurt. Get your drawers on and go see." Nancy hurried to the kitchen to heat some water.

Moments later, Ian joined Adam in the alley. "Where is he, lad?"

"This way. In the shack. He's all bloodied. I think he's dead."

When Ian entered and saw Jeremy on the floor, he realized Adam had not been exaggerating. Jeremy's crumpled form was ominously still.

"Hold the light while I get these ropes undone." Ian worked feverishly as he mumbled, "Och laddie, what have ye got yourself into. God let him be all right."

Jeremy groaned.

"He's alive. Thank God. Just lie still laddie."

Jeremy tried to speak but failed.

"Adam, go fetch Meggie and they physician, Mr. Coomb. Quickly!"

Adam disappeared.

As he had so many times before, Ian carried Jeremy into the tavern and down the hall to his bedroom.

Nancy came in and placed a basin of water on the table as Ian stepped back from the bed. Looking at Jeremy's bloodied face,

Nancy put her hand over her mouth and cried out, "God in heaven! The laddie's dead!"

"Hush, woman. He's no dead, but almost. See if you can clean him up."

Tears rolled down Nancy's face, as she gently wiped the blood from Jeremy's wounds.

"Here," said Ian, handing a folded cloth to Nancy. "You'll be needin' to staunch the blood with this. Be careful of his left arm."

"Oh, laddie, who would do such a thing to ye? Poor bonnie laddie. I can no recognize ye."

Meggie burst through the door. "Oh God, what's happened?" Seeing the swollen black and blue face and bloodied water, Meggie blanched and screamed.

"Whist, child. Ye'll be no good to him like that," Ian scolded gently.

Clutching her breast, Meggie approached the bed and knelt beside Jeremy's head. Gingerly, she reached out and touched his face. His skin was cold. Tears streamed down her face as she turned to her mother. "Is he alive?"

"Barely. Is Mr. Coomb on his way?"

"Adam s ... s ... said he was g ... goin' to g ... get him," Meggie stammered out between sobs. "What happened to him, Daddy?"

"We don't know for sure, lassie. Adam thought he heard some noises comin' from yon shack near the stables and when he went to look, he found Jeremy lyin' there. Like as not, some scoundrels beat him up and left him for dead. How he got there is a mystery."

"When I left, he said he was going to get to sleep early. We were joking about how the women were running his life." Meggie's hands were shaking. "I didn't disturb him when I went up to bed. They must've come here after him. But why?"

"That is the question, Meggie," replied Ian. "Did he never tell you anything about why he was here before and lookin' so different?

"No, he said I had to trust him that he wasn't doing anything bad." Meggie sobbed again. "Jemmy. Jemmy. Can you hear me, luv?" she called softly, putting her face close to his. "Jemmy, it's me, Meggie. Can you hear me? Oh my darling Jemmy. My love." Fresh tears flowed and dropped on Jeremy's cheek.

A feeble moan escaped his lips.

"Jemmy! It's all right, luv. You're going to be all right. The physician's coming to help you. My love, oh my darlin'."

There was a light knock on the door, followed by the entrance of the disheveled, rotund figure of Mr. Coomb. "What's all this about? Couldn't make any sense out of that boy." On reaching the bed, Mr. Coomb sucked in his breath. "God in heaven!"

"Please help him, Mr. Coomb. We're to be married soon."

"If you ladies will move aside ..."

Meggie and Nancy joined Ian by the table. Mr. Coomb gently lifted Jeremy's eyelids, released them and drew back on his knees, listening to his raspy breathing. A gurgling noise was coming from Jeremy's throat and blood coursed from his mouth. Reluctantly, Mr. Coomb stood and faced the expectant trio. He shook his head. "I'm sorry. He's badly hurt inside. There's nothing I can do," he said sadly.

Nancy turned to Ian's waiting arms as Meggie cried out and ran to the physician. "You must do something! You must! You must!" she screamed, pounding Mr. Coomb on the chest. His portly arms encircled her. "We're to be wed. We're to be ..." Her voice became muffled in his jacket as tears and sobs wrenched her body.

Suddenly, she broke away from him and ran to Jeremy. "You can't die! You can't! My love! My love." Reaching under his back, she pulled his head to her breast, stroked his bloody hair and rocked him back and forth. "It's all right. You're going to be all right."

Mr. Coomb looked at the McIntoshes, shook his head again and quietly went out the door. Tears flowed from Ian and Nancy, as they stood holding each other and looking at their distraught daughter. They turned and followed the doctor.

Meggie continued rocking Jeremy and softly crooned her words, "Never mind, Jeremy. It'll be all right. Meggie's here. I'll love you forever. We'll always be together, luv."

Like a sigh carried on the wind, she heard a whisper, "Some day."

𝔈𝔭𝔦𝔩𝔬𝔤𝔲𝔢

1594

Leaves whispered to one another as the gentle breeze blew softly through the trees. The July sunlight was not strong enough to cause discomfort, although it is doubtful if the young woman sitting on the carpet of green, staring at the headstone, would have noticed, so lost in memories was she. Perhaps visions of Jeremy and the way their life might have been were replacing the words which marked his death.

She absent-mindedly twisted the ruby and diamond ring on her left hand, as alternating emotions of happiness and sorrow played across her face, much as the waves ebb and flow across the endless ocean.

Jeremy Hawkins June15,1565 - May 27, 1589

Beloved husband of Meghan Sept. 9, 1567 -

Sister of Catherine and Brother of

Capt. John Hawkins Nov. 7, 1559 - Nov. 30, 1591

Meggie stood up and looked back through the trees to Hawkesbury Manor. Her twin boys, so like their father, would be missing her. She turned, laid a hand on the headstone and spoke softly. "You would be so proud of our sons, Jeremy. Some day I'll tell them about you. About us."

A breeze caressed her cheek. "Some day ..."